FINDING THEIR WAY

Attempting to shake off writer's block, novelist Fran Miller comes to the Cornish village of Tresidder to spend the summer with her long-time best friend, Lucy. She definitely isn't looking for romance, especially after a painful breakup with her last boyfriend — but it finds her nevertheless in the form of Charlie Boscawen, local baker and heart-throb. Soon she is being wooed with the most tempting confections imaginable. But Charlie has problems of his own . . . and what will happen when the summer comes to an end?

Books by Angela Britnell
in the Linford Romance Library:

HUSHED WORDS
FLAMES THAT MELT
SICILIAN ESCAPE
CALIFORNIA DREAMING
A SMOKY MOUNTAIN CHRISTMAS
ENDLESS LOVE
HOME AT LAST
AN UNEXPECTED LOVE
WHERE WE BELONG
WISHES CAN COME TRUE
HOLIDAY HOPES
WHAT HAPPENS IN NASHVILLE
THE WEDDING REJECT TABLE
YOU'RE THE ONE THAT I WANT

ANGELA BRITNELL

FINDING
THEIR WAY

Complete and Unabridged

LINFORD
Leicester

First published in Great Britain in 2017

First Linford Edition
published 2018

A catalogue record for this book is available
from the British Library.

ISBN 978–1–4448–3810–7

Published by
F. A. Thorpe (Publishing)
Anstey, Leicestershire

Set by Words & Graphics Ltd.
Anstey, Leicestershire
Printed and bound in Great Britain by
T. J. International Ltd., Padstow, Cornwall

This book is printed on acid-free paper

1

'Your Charlie is as nice as he looks, but you'll be wasting your time like the rest of us. He's married to his cakes!'

A ripple of laughter broke through Fran's musing and she jerked around to face the grey-haired woman behind her in the shop queue. 'Excuse me?'

'I couldn't help notice you drooling over Cornwall's answer to Paul Holly-wood.'

Fran's cheeks burned. 'I'm sorry, but I've no clue what you're talking about.' Not strictly true, because she *had* been staring at the handsome man serving behind the counter. Despite officially leaving all interest in men behind in California, his deep soft voice, thick blond wavy hair, and simple white T-shirt stretched over broad shoulders had stirred her interest.

'You're not from around these parts, are you?'

Fran shook her head, wishing now she'd let her friend do the shopping instead.

'I don't suppose you've seen the popular baking show I'm talking about?'

'No.' She wished she could end the discussion without being rude, but the woman launched into a lengthy description of a cookery programme that apparently had the nation enthralled. Why would watching people bake cakes make riveting viewing?

'You'll be in big trouble if your sponge has a soggy bottom.'

It was all Fran could do not to burst out laughing, but her newfound acquaintance looked deadly serious.

'Mary Berry always catches them out.' She nodded her approval. 'And as for Paul . . . '

Maybe they'd finally get to the man whose name started this bizarre interlude.

'All the women swoon over his searing blue eyes.' The woman sighed happily. 'He's a bit stern too.' The implication was, *And don't we all like that in a man.* 'Listen to me rattling on. My Jeb always says I can talk the hind legs off a donkey. Oh, you're next, love. I'm Edna Kittow, by the way.'

Clearly Fran was expected to answer and satisfy the woman's curiosity. A flutter of panic clutched at her throat.

'What can I get for you today?' Charlie didn't want to startle the pretty dark-haired woman seemingly frozen in front of him. 'Are you looking for something in particular?' The other customers were staring at them. Suddenly a touch of awareness crept into her startling jade-green eyes.

'I'm sorry. Did you say something?'

He caught a trace of an accent in her soft voice but couldn't immediately place it. Charlie repeated his earlier questions and she pulled a scrap of paper from the pocket of her denim jacket and thrust it across the counter at him. He immediately recognised the writing.

'Mrs. Hunt's usual. No problem.' The doctor's wife bought the same things every Friday: a ham and Gruyere quiche, a chocolate Swiss roll, and a dozen plain scones. He considered asking where Lucy Hunt was today but instead simply got the order ready and set the paper bags down on the glass countertop.

'Lucy said that would cover it.' She passed a twenty-pound note across to him. 'I hope she's right, because I don't have any more money.'

'I can always put you to washing dishes in the kitchen,' Charlie joked, and the merest hint of a smile pulled at her mouth. 'Don't worry, you get away with it this time.' He opened the till to get some change and dropped it into her outstretched hand.

'Thank you for your . . . kindness.'

'My pleasure.' As he held her gaze, Charlie felt the heat rising in his neck. 'Take care.'

The woman nodded and left the shop before he could make a fool of himself. For the rest of the afternoon he stayed busy, but when Charlie turned over the sign to Closed at five o'clock, he was filled with an unwelcome restlessness.

What he *wanted* to do was take his long-neglected sports car out for a run down the coast. What he *would* do was go back home and cook dinner for his parents, as usual. Five o'clock in the morning rolled around quickly, and if he didn't get an early night, Charlie would be dragging tomorrow.

Soon enough, he'd hear on the village grapevine who the skittish young woman was connected to Dr. Hunt. No story went untold in Tresidder.

★ ★ ★

'Did you see our village heartthrob?'

'Is the doctor that popular?' Fran pretended to misunderstand her long-time best friend.

'Hardly!' Lucy roared with laughter.

'Except with me of course.' Her eyes narrowed. 'Oh, you're a clever girl. Poor Charlie. Another member for his fan club.'

Charlie. Yeah, the name suits him. Fun. Easygoing. The complete opposite of me.

'I guess you're talking about the pleasant man who served me in the shop?'

'Pleasant? Do you need your eyesight checked?' Lucy scoffed. 'Even respectable married women like me have a quiet swoon over Charlie.' Her expression softened. 'Did I touch a nerve? I'm sorry. I thought he might make a good hero for your next book, but don't you dare turn him into one of your gruesome dead bodies,' she warned.

'I promise I won't.' Fran plastered on a bright smile. 'Why don't you tell me about the job you've got lined up for me?' She swiftly steered the conversation away from her writing and men — both sore subjects at the moment.

Reading an Agatha Christie biography had sparked the idea of taking a break from her life. When the world-famous writer disappeared for eleven days in 1926, she'd been working too hard, and was grieving over her mother's recent death and upset by problems in her marriage. The similarities were eerie, except in Fran's case it was a disloyal boyfriend instead of a husband.

'Just remember, if you want to talk I'm a good listener.' Lucy smiled. 'I know we haven't seen each other in years, but we used to share everything.'

'The job?'

'I'm wondering now if it's suitable. You said you'd do anything for the summer, but . . . ' A deep frown settled on her forehead.

'I meant it.'

'Don't take this the wrong way, but you don't seem very comfortable around people these days, not even me.' Lucy touched her arm. 'We can easily get someone else. It was simply that you rang on the very day — '

'Spit it out. Please.'

'I had a little scare the other day with the baby.' Lucy patted her rounded stomach. 'Truthfully, it frightened Patrick more, because doctors never do well if someone they care for is ill. He wants me to give up being his receptionist for a while and take it easy for the rest of the pregnancy. We were going to advertise for some temporary help until after the baby's born and I decide if I'm going back to work.'

'That'll suit me perfectly.' A small doctor's office in a tiny Cornish village should be quiet and undemanding — exactly what she needed. With any luck, being in quiet Tresidder for the summer might spark book number eleven in her Calendar Corpses series and get that side of her life back on track.

'If you're sure?'

'Absolutely.' Fran hoped she sounded convincing. 'When do I start?'

'We can visit the surgery over the weekend to go through the routine while there aren't any patients around, and then we'll work together on Monday and see how you get on.'

'Right. Now why don't you sit down and I'll make us a cup of tea,' Fran offered.

'Lovely. I'll have mine with a large slice of Swiss roll while Patrick's not around to tell me off,' Lucy said with a grin. 'When you've tasted Charlie's divine baking, you might change your mind about him.'

It would take more than a perfect sponge cake to win her over.

2

Charlie finished working on the shop accounts and slipped off his glasses, dropping them on the table with a heavy sigh. Profits were up on last year and the summer weather forecast was good, which would mean more visitors and more sales. After his brother's death, he'd reluctantly come home to take over the struggling family business and in two short years turned Boscawen's Bites around. Alex had been a good baker but a terrible businessman. Charlie still made a lot of the traditional favourites, but had cut out the time-consuming bread-making and expanded the deli side of the business. Over the upcoming winter, he had plans for a major renovation of the shop to expand the café.

You turn everything to gold, Charlie boy.

Alex's half-joking, half-bitter words haunted him. Logically he knew it wasn't his fault, but twins were supposed to always be there for each other, and Charlie failed his brother when it counted the most. He'd been chasing his dream in London and on the cusp of fame, poised to be awarded the third Michelin star for his restaurant, when everything fell apart.

'Charlie, is it cocoa time?' His mother's voice drifted in from the other room and he took a few steadying breaths before replying.

'Yes, Mum. I'll put the kettle on.'

His village reputation as a far too handsome man who dished out cheeky winks and flattery along with his delicious scones allowed him the freedom to live his life the way he needed to right now. He closed down his laptop.

'I don't suppose you brought any seed buns home?'

He gritted his teeth, determined not to snap at his father. George Boscawen knew seed buns were one of the items Charlie had slashed from the menu, but persisted in asking for them. From the time he was sixteen, George had worked in the bakery that Charlie's great-grandfather had started back in the 1920s. Unfortunately, he'd been forced to take early retirement ten years ago due to the painful arthritis riddling his body.

'How about a saffron bun instead? They're fresh today.'

'You know fresh ones give me indigestion,' he complained. 'I suppose I'll have one of those newfangled muffins. Stupid name for a sweet bun.'

Charlie didn't bother trying to explain because he'd be wasting his breath. The words 'changing with the times' weren't in his father's vocabulary. He quietly started to get their supper ready and relaxed a little when his father left the kitchen.

'Here we go.' He set everything down on the table in front of the sofa and picked up his own mug of coffee. 'I'm going outside for a while. It's a nice evening.'

'That's right, leave us alone as usual,' George grumbled.

'I could do with a bit of fresh air, that's all.' At nearly forty, he shouldn't have to justify himself to his parents. In another year the business should be financially stable enough for him to look at buying his own house again. Charlie missed his London flat in the Docklands area with its stunning view over the Thames, but it'd been sold to finance improvements to the building when he first took over the business. He could afford to rent something now, but in his eyes that was throwing money away.

'I've been stuck in the shop all day. You know what that's like.' A flash of pain crossed his father's face and Charlie could've kicked himself. It'd been hard enough when George was forced to turn over the business to Alex, but things became worse within a few short years when the bakery was teetering on the edge of bankruptcy. 'Sorry, Dad. I didn't mean — '

'Do what you like,' his father growled, and turned his attention back to the newspaper.

Charlie grabbed his mug and hurried through the kitchen. He flung open the back door and stepped outside with a surge of relief, easing himself into one of the flimsy red and white folding chairs that weren't designed for someone his size. He had offered to buy new ones, but his father had only mocked his supposed extravagance.

You've been up country too long and picked up London ways. We don't fritter our money away here. The chairs still work. They'll do.

He hadn't argued because it would've been pointless. Charlie dragged his thoughts away from his intractable father and allowed them to linger on something far more agreeable.

Little Miss Mystery. He'd tagged the woman that way because so many

14

things about her didn't make sense. Her short black hair seemed to have been hacked off with garden shears, and the cheap baggy jeans, T-shirt and worn denim jacket all indicated a woman who didn't care much for outward appearance. But despite that, she carried her tall frame with a striking elegance, and her golden lightly tanned skin and clear jade-green eyes told a different story.

Charlie sipped his coffee and wondered.

★   ★   ★

Lucy stopped in the middle of explaining the appointments system. 'Fran ... don't get me wrong, because it's great to see you, but what went wrong in Los Angeles? I thought you'd be working on your next bestseller, not taking the summer off to hang out in Cornwall with us.'

The minute she got off the train, Fran knew coming to see her old friend was a mistake. She wouldn't be able to fool Lucy. They'd met at primary school in Plymouth when they were eight and been inseparable for the next five years. Their fathers were both stationed at the nearby naval base, which made a natural dividing line between them and the 'genuine' local children. When the inevitable happened and Fran's family relocated to Portsmouth, the friendship naturally faded because making new best friends was a fact of forces life. Somehow they'd stayed on the periphery of each other's existence and ended up back at university together in Plymouth.

'Come on. Remember our wine-drinking, chocolate-eating, and put-the-world-to-rights sessions?' Lucy pleaded. 'Nothing you say will go any further than this room.'

'Oh, Lucy, don't be daft.' Fran shook her head. 'We both know you'll have to share it with Patrick . . . and that's right.' She hurried on before her old friend could protest. 'That's the way it should be. You'll have to accept that I'm okay.' Fran managed a wry smile. 'Not amazing. Not exceptional. But okay.'

'Losing your mum must've been hard. How's your dad getting on?'

Fran shrugged. 'All right I guess. He's got his work and a good circle of friends from living in Monterey nearly fifteen years. He could retire but isn't really ready yet, and the aquarium isn't in a hurry to let him go.' Her father had been lured to work in America after he'd retired from the Royal Navy because of his oceanographic expertise, and she'd joined her parents there after she graduated from university.

'I might resort to bribing you with one of Charlie's cakes to drag the full story out of you after the way you inhaled that Swiss roll.'

Fran couldn't resist laughing along with Lucy. 'If anything could do the trick, that might,' she admitted. 'They're pretty exceptional.' Not normally much of a cake lover, she thought she'd died and gone to heaven when she took her first bite of the soft rich sponge and thick vanilla-laced cream.

'So is Charlie. It's a pity he . . . doesn't get to show off his cooking talents to a wider audience.'

Her reticence aroused Fran's curiosity. 'Presumably he could leave Tresidder if he wanted.'

'Not really. Charlie's great-grandfather started the family business back in the 1920s and there's no one else left to run it.' Lucy shrugged. 'I'm being silly. There's no reason not to tell you more. When Patrick and I moved here ten years ago, George Boscawen had just retired because of ill health and turned over the business to Charlie's twin brother, Alex. Charlie was running his own successful restaurant in London, but came back about two years ago when Alex was killed in a car crash in France.'

'That's awful.'

'Yes. Everyone feels sorry for him, although he'd hate to hear me say so.' Lucy held up a warning finger. 'Don't

18

tell Patrick we've discussed Charlie, because they're good mates.'

'See, this is what happens when you start to keep secrets.' Fran touched her friend's hand.

'It's not a secret,' Lucy protested. 'It's common knowledge around Tresidder.' Her cheeks heated. 'Patrick simply hates gossip. I suppose it comes from being a doctor. He has to be scrupulous about not discussing his patients, and it runs over into other aspects of his life. He's a bit obsessive, to be honest.'

'It's all right. I won't say anything. I was a bit curious, that's all.'

Lucy grinned. 'I'm glad. If you weren't, I'd know there was something seriously wrong with you.'

'Not that serious!' There would surely be few women who didn't find Charlie attractive, and she certainly wasn't one of them. That didn't mean she intended to act on it. 'Anyway, back to business. What do I need to wear for work?' A touch of relief crossed her friend's face. 'I do have some better things with me.'

'Good. Maybe we can look at them together later?'

'Perfect.' Not really, but she'd let herself in for this and would follow through. Lucy and Patrick were helping her out by letting her stay over the summer, so this was the least she could do in return. 'Why don't you go over the filing system again with me?'

They got back to work, but Fran knew her friend wasn't finished with her yet.

3

'Sorry, I'm about to close. There's nothing much left, I'm afraid, apart from a few fruit scones. You can have them half price,' Charlie explained to the man who walked in, continuing to wipe down the counter. Possibly American, judging by the buzz cut hair, wraparound sunglasses and gleaming white teeth.

'I guess you know everyone around here?' the man asked, his deep drawl confirming Charlie's intuition.

'Most of the locals I do, but we've a lot of tourists like yourself.'

'I'm not a tourist. I'm here on business and heard that a friend of mine might be in the area. She hasn't been well recently, and I thought I'd check on her if she's around.'

'I haven't seen any other Americans this week.' Not an outright lie or the complete truth. Charlie only picked up the hint of an accent in his mystery customer that he couldn't *swear* had been American. 'What's her name? It might ring a bell.'

'Francesca Miller, but she usually goes by Fran. She's tall and very striking.' He turned his phone screen towards Charlie. 'That's a recent photo.'

Despite the woman's long brunette hair, he immediately recognised his mystery customer. 'Sorry. Can't help you.'

The man opened his wallet and pulled out a business card. 'If you see her, please get in touch.' He passed it over the counter. 'I'll make it worth your while.'

Charlie fingered the card. *Randy Seacrest. Literary agent, Los Angeles, California.* 'You must be close friends to go to all this trouble, Mr Seacrest.'

'Oh, yeah, we're definitely that. We go back years.' Something about the seemingly casual reply made Charlie uneasy. 'Thanks, pal.'

He watched the man leave and wondered whether to mention Seacrest's visit to Patrick later.

★ ★ ★

'Do you fancy venturing out for a drink?' Lucy asked, coming in from the kitchen. 'Patrick's going down to the Green Man and I thought we might join him.'

'Why don't you two go without me and have some time on your own? I'm quite content to stay here and read.'

'Don't be silly. My beloved hubby plays snooker most Saturday evenings with the gorgeous Charlie, which means if I go and none of my friends are there, I'm left alone to sip orange juice and twiddle my thumbs.'

'I don't know. I — '

'Don't be so suspicious!' Lucy laughed. 'I'm not trying to pair the two of you off. Look on it as preparation for Monday. You can dip your toes in the water and meet a few people.'

Fran's stomach knotted. What had she expected? To live like a hermit at the bottom of Lucy's garden while she waited for her literary muse to return? She met her friend's encouraging smile and couldn't see any way out. 'Sure. We'll go.'

'Good. I'm going to change out of these old leggings and see if I can squeeze into something a bit smarter.'

'You look wonderful.' She wasn't exaggerating. Lucy was one of the lucky women who blossomed in pregnancy and had never looked better. By Patrick's frequent admiring glances, it was obvious he thought so too.

'How about you?'

'In what way?'

'I know it's only the local pub, but . . . '

Fran became aware of her ugly clothes coming under scrutiny and failing some unspoken test. 'Fine. I'll change too.'

'Do you have anything that actually

fits?' Lucy blurted out, and two heated red circles appeared on her cheeks. 'I'm sorry, but you were always smartly dressed and into the latest fashions. And this?' She perched on the sofa next to her and touched Fran's cropped, badly dyed hair. 'Why?'

It would sound absurd to say she'd done it all to avoid being recognised. When a woman was nearly six feet tall with her distinctive features, blending in was almost impossible.

'I only mean . . . I'm worried about you. You've been so quiet since you arrived. I wish you could tell me everything that's wrong.'

'So do I,' she whispered. 'So do I.' They leaned in closer and their foreheads touched. 'But I can't. Not yet.' Fran eased back to meet her friend's sympathetic gaze. 'Until then, it won't kill me to put on a pair of decent jeans and break out the lipstick.'

'We don't have to go out if you really don't want to.'

'Nope. We're going.' Fran jumped up.

'Whenever you're ready to leave the pub, you only have to say.'

Ten minutes after they got there would suit her perfectly, but that wasn't likely to happen.

★　★　★

Charlie nearly choked on his beer. His anonymous stranger, lovelier than he remembered, was walking towards him. He hopped down off the bar stool as Patrick reached him first and they shook hands.

'How's it going, mate? Long week?'

'Could say that.' Patrick chuckled and rolled his eyes at his wife. 'This one doesn't trust me. She's come to keep an eye on us tonight.'

'Quite right, too. Lucy's a wise woman,' Charlie teased, all the while trying not to stare at the woman holding back and making no move to join in the conversation.

'This is our friend, Fran Miller, who's over from California and staying with us for the summer.' Patrick tugged at her arm and she reluctantly came closer.

'Charlie Boscawen. Pleased to meet you . . . again.'

She stared at his outstretched hand for a couple of seconds before giving it a brief shake.

Patrick frowned. 'Where did you — '

'At the shop,' Charlie interrupted. 'She was after one of my Swiss rolls.'

'All the women are, from what I hear,' he jibed. 'The Cake Romeo, that's my old friend.'

Charlie dredged up a smile.

'Leave him alone,' Lucy chided her husband. 'Go and play snooker so we can have a good gossip.'

'As long as it's not about us.'

'Good heavens, I hope we'll find something far more interesting to talk about,' she scoffed. 'Don't you, Fran?'

'Maybe.' The slight amused lilt to her voice brought out the hint of an accent Charlie had picked up on before. Her eyes shone as they rested on him, and he held her gaze longer than he should. Today's dark jeans and black scoop-neck T-shirt fitted better, but he guessed they were still chosen with the idea of rendering her inconspicuous. They failed miserably, because nothing could disguise her natural beauty. The tempting slick of deep pink lip gloss enhancing her generous mouth gave her away by telling him that she wasn't as indifferent to her looks as she wanted everyone to believe.

'I'll get the drinks in,' he said. 'What will it be, ladies?'

Lucy wrinkled up her nose. 'Another boring orange juice for me and the little one.' She tenderly rested her hand on her stomach and glanced lovingly at Patrick.

'Certainly.' He glanced over at Fran, taken aback by the film of tears shimmering in her eyes. Charlie laid his hand gently on her arm. 'For you?'

'Red wine, please.' Her voice wasn't quite steady. 'Merlot if they have it.'

'No problem. Why don't you and

Lucy sit down and we'll bring the drinks over?' He smiled. 'I promise we'll leave you alone then.'

'Don't feel you have to rush off. I don't bite.' Her beguiling smile reeled Charlie in. 'Unless it's one of your Swiss rolls; and as Patrick said, that's a different story.' A flush of heat raced up her neck. 'Forget that; I didn't mean — '

'It's all right,' he politely cut off her attempt to apologise. 'I'm always pleased to hear someone enjoys my baking.' He became aware that he was still touching her arm and took a step backwards. 'Patrick. Drinks?'

'Good idea. A man could die of thirst around here.'

Up at the bar, Charlie placed their order and wondered how best to ask the question niggling at his brain. Before he could open his mouth, Patrick wagged his finger.

'Stay clear of Fran, mate. I don't know any details, but she's got some problems going on in her life. That's why she's here.'

Charlie held up his hands. 'Hey, I'm not going there. Don't worry. But listen to this.' He started to tell Patrick about Randy Seacrest's visit, and his friend's face darkened.

4

'I don't bite. Unless it's one of your Swiss rolls?' Lucy mimicked her and raised a questioning eyebrow. 'For someone who's not interested, that sounded suspiciously like flirting to me.'

Fran couldn't tell her friend yet another lie. 'It wasn't intentional, but he's fun and good-looking, and I'm human.'

'Well, that's a relief.' Lucy grinned. 'Now I feel I haven't totally lost my old friend after all.'

A pang of remorse clutched at Fran.

'I knew she was in there somewhere,' Lucy carried on. 'Word of warning. As I said, Charlie flirts. He's friendly with everyone, but that's as far as it goes.'

'I guess he's got his reasons,' Fran couldn't resist probing.

'Several. I don't — '

'There you go.' Patrick announced and set down their drinks. 'One wine and one orange juice. Charlie's bringing the crisps and peanuts.' He grinned at Lucy. 'I told him you can't go longer than an hour these days without eating.'

'Isn't my husband the sweetest man?' She playfully stuck out her tongue.

Yes, he really is, and you're lucky. I know you're joking and so does he. That's such a gift. Fran glanced up and caught Charlie watching her with unmistakeable sympathy. Other people might mark him down as cheerful and an incorrigible flirt, but she suspected there was far more to him lurking under the surface.

Charlie dumped a pile of snack bags in the middle of the table. 'We'll leave you to it. Behave yourselves.'

'Boring,' Fran retorted.

'That's me. Mr. Boring . . . most of the time.' He aimed a long, slow wink at her and strolled away.

'OMG. Forget everything I said.' Lucy sighed. 'Why not enjoy a little flirtation if it's on offer? He's got a cute little red sports car too, which could be an added lure, because I remember your dad getting you hooked on cars. Summers are supposed to be about having fun.' She patted her stomach. 'There's a limit to how much fun I can have, so this way I can experience some second-hand.'

Fran shook her head. 'Oh no. I'm not providing your entertainment for the next few months. Charlie Boscawen is the absolute last thing I need.' *And I'm the absolute last thing he needs.*

'We'll see.' Her friend's smug expression spoke volumes. She selected a packet of crisps and popped them open.

'Salt and vinegar still?'

'Is there any other kind?' Lucy grabbed several and crammed them into her mouth. Her inability to resist the tangy crisps used to be a running joke between them. Whatever diet she was on at the time, they were always her downfall.

'Good?'

Lucy snorted. 'Good doesn't begin to describe them. Try some. They're much safer than flirting with Charlie.'

Anything would be. Driving without a seatbelt. Getting caught in a tornado. Being lost at sea. Fran smiled and reached for a bag. 'Let's see if you're right.'

★ ★ ★

'Are you going to tell her?' Charlie asked, sizing up the table and getting ready to annihilate Patrick for the sixth week in a row. His old friend was a great doctor but an indifferent snooker player. Occasionally he managed to win if Charlie was having an off week, but that wouldn't be the case tonight.

'I'll mention it to Lucy later and see what she thinks.'

'Good move, exactly like this,' he quipped and proceeded to sink the last three balls. Charlie stuck out his hand. 'Five pounds.'

'Call yourself a mate?' Patrick

groused and fished out his wallet.

'I can't help it if you're useless,' he laughed, and snatched the money from his friend's hand. 'Look at it this way — the Lifeboat Society does well out of you! I'm pretty sure you've bought them a whole boat on your own by now.' Charlie piled on the friendly abuse. He made his way over to the bar and stuck the money in the charity box.

'You staying for another drink?' Patrick asked.

'Better not. I ought to head home.'

'It's your day off tomorrow. Live dangerously.'

Charlie didn't want to be a drag, but his old friend didn't get it. A few years ago he'd willingly worked fourteen-hour days at his restaurant but still found time for an active social life. Now he was lucky to snatch a few minutes to read the newspaper before falling asleep at night, ready to do it all over again the next day.

'I don't mean to be an insensitive clod,' Patrick apologised. 'How about coming over for dinner with us one night this week? Surely your parents can manage on their own for once?' He persisted, 'I'll ask what day's good for Lucy and give you a ring.'

Despite his misgivings, Charlie agreed. 'Say good night to the girls for me.' If he stupidly went over himself, he'd get tempted to stay and flirt with Fran. She'd give him that tempting look again, making him itch to throw all idea of caution away. 'Bye.'

He wended his way through the packed Saturday-night crowd and stepped outside with a sense of having dodged a bullet. He decided to take a short cut through the nearby park and disturbed a pair of disgruntled teenagers sneaking a quick smoke and a stray cat rummaging through the overflowing rubbish bin. Within sight of home, he sat down on an empty bench and rested his hands on his outstretched legs. He shouldn't have agreed to Patrick's offer and needed to come up with a plausible excuse.

Although it was only early June, business was cranking up for the summer, and it wouldn't be a complete lie to say he didn't have the time. If they waited until the holiday crowds left, then Francesca Miller would've gone too, and he'd be safe from his foolish longings.

He heaved himself to his feet and strolled across the deserted street. He shoved in his key and noticed the front door needed a fresh coat of black paint.

'At last.' His father appeared in the kitchen doorway. 'You've got some explaining to do. What's all this about?' he barked, waving an envelope in Charlie's face.

He spotted the French stamp and his heart sank. 'Opening my private post now?' he went on the offensive.

'I didn't open it and I wouldn't have understood a word anyway. You promised us you wouldn't contact that woman.' He spat out the last two words. His contempt for Chantelle Bonet never wavered.

'Strictly speaking, she contacted me first.'

'But you replied.'

'Yes, I did,' Charlie answered back. He stepped closer and smelled the lingering odour of whisky on his father's breath. 'What're you going to do about it?'

'That creature as good as killed your brother,' he hissed.

'Don't be ridiculous. You're the only one who believes that.'

'Your mother — '

'Pretends to agree with you to keep the peace.'

'Don't you dare talk about her that way.'

'It's the truth,' Charlie said. 'I'm not a child. You can't order me around anymore.' He'd backed down too often, but it wasn't happening tonight. 'I'm going to bed.'

'What about this?' George shoved the letter at him.

'I'll take it.' He snatched the envelope away. 'Good night.' Charlie took the stairs two at a time and dived into his bedroom, slamming the door shut behind him. Sitting on the bed, he yanked out the thin blue sheets of airmail paper and scanned over the first page, translating in his head as he went. He hadn't wanted to believe her absurd claim, but now she'd sent him the proof.

Alexandre Bonet-Boscawen.

He handled the small photograph gingerly, tracing his fingers over the child's thick blond hair and registering the luminous sky-blue eyes and long, incongruously dark lashes. The same features Charlie saw reflected in the mirror every day and that he'd shared with Alex. The little boy would never know his father, but that didn't mean the rest of his English family needed to be strangers. He owed Alex better than that.

By the time he finished reading, Charlie could hardly focus through the tears clouding his eyes. He'd have to think carefully before he replied.

5

Fran allowed herself a tiny smile. The simple navy linen skirt, white blouse, and flat navy sandals screamed 'respectable doctor's receptionist' — at least, that was how she'd dress a character in this situation.

A tremor of unease kicked aside her good humour. *New York Times* bestselling author or not, if she couldn't get the right patient files to Patrick and juggle the appointments schedule today, she'd be a failure.

Take a deep breath. Slowly, in and out. Push away all negative thoughts. You can do this.

'Are you ready?' Lucy shouted up the stairs. 'Patrick's going to give us a lift.'

Fran would have preferred to walk, but the surgery was at the top of Pondhu Hill, the steepest road in

Tresidder, and Patrick was concerned about his wife. Overly so, according to Lucy. But who could blame him? 'Coming.'

'Gosh, you're looking smart.' Lucy beamed as Fran made her way down the stairs.

'Don't sound so surprised. You helped me pick it out.'

'I know, but I think I'd forgotten how . . . good you can look.'

'Ready, ladies?' Patrick's welcome interruption came at the perfect time. 'Word of warning, Fran. Make the most of the relative quiet today, because tomorrow morning the phone won't stop ringing.'

'Why's that?'

He chuckled. 'The word will get around, and they'll all want to check out my new receptionist.' A touch of warning darkened his eyes. 'You'd better have a story ready, because they're bound to ask where you're from and why you're here.'

'Don't put her off.' Lucy glared at

her husband. 'Don't worry,' she hastened to reassure Fran. 'Give a brief polite explanation and make it clear that's all they'll get.'

'Not a problem,' she declared, far more confidently than she felt.

Morning surgery started at half past eight and in theory lasted for three hours, but it was gone noon before they were through.

'Finally.' Lucy pushed her chair away from the desk. 'Lunch time. Well, for us it is. Patrick will be leaving to do his home visits in a minute.'

'Won't he be hungry?'

'He keeps a tin of peanuts and some dried fruit in the car for emergencies. Someone usually takes pity and offers him a cup of tea along the way.' Lucy grinned. 'He's also been known to stop at the shop to buy a pasty or sneak in a sandwich at the Green Man if he's got any spare time.' Her smile lost some of its vibrancy. 'Of course, he works too hard. Do you know he was up at six this morning to catch up on paperwork and return patient phone calls before we even had our breakfast? I doubt he'll be finished much before seven tonight.'

'Is my beautiful wife spinning you a load of nonsense about me being a saint?' Patrick joked as he came out from his office carrying his medical bag. 'I gripe about red tape and annoying patients, but I love my job. Couldn't imagine doing anything else.'

Fran envied his focus and certainty. Once she'd had the same joy in her writing. As a new author, it'd been a thrill to get a twelve-book contract for her Calendar Corpses series; and when they took off and sold more than she could've ever imagined, she had been euphoric. But the burden of her fans' expectations wore her down; and after the tenth book, *Ordeal in October*, soared up the bestseller charts and stayed there for weeks, it all became too much. Plus there'd been Randy. But if she started to think about him now, she'd never survive the day.

'Behave yourselves,' Patrick said,

giving them a cheery wave as he left.

'God, I'm starving,' Lucy exclaimed. 'I usually pack a sandwich but I forgot this morning.'

'Do you want me to run down to the village and buy us something?' Fran seized on the chance to get out.

'That would be great. I always take a break now and start work again around one. I answer the phones and do admin stuff until afternoon surgery starts at three.'

'What do you fancy eating?'

'A horse?' Lucy joked. 'If that's not an option, go to Charlie's and get me a five-grain baguette with tuna, cucumber, rocket and extra garlic lemon mayonnaise — make sure it's a full-size one, not the wimpy half version. Toss in some of his amazing potato salad and a large lemonade as well. If you happen to sneak in a couple of white chocolate almond cookies, I'll love you forever. They are absolutely to die for.'

'How many babies are you feeding in there?' Fran playfully touched her friend's stomach, squashing a surge of envy.

'You're as bad as Patrick. Wait until it's your turn.'

'That's never going to happen.' The words tumbled out before Fran could stop them.

'You don't know that. You've been unlucky with men, that's all.'

No, it's not all. She'd go along with her friend's theory, because the alternative was to share the whole painful story. 'Maybe.' She checked the clock and snatched up her handbag. 'I'd better hurry up. I don't want you fading away.' She quickly stepped out of the surgery and headed down the hill, unable to help smiling at the prospect of seeing Charlie again.

★   ★   ★

The Grab 'n' Go Lunches were a hit, and Charlie couldn't make them fast enough. He'd taken the mix-and-match idea popular in other shops and elevated it, complete with a recyclable cardboard picnic basket. At this rate, he'd soon be able to increase Robbie Giles from four days a week up to full time. Lots of people said he was mad to employ the troublesome teenager, but Charlie had seen echoes of himself in the sometimes surly, difficult boy. Meeting everyone's low expectations became a habit if it wasn't redirected. Thankfully, he'd found his home in the kitchen, and he'd seen encouraging signs of the same thing happening to Robbie.

'You want me to go out back and make more sandwiches or serve this customer, Mr. B?' Robbie asked.

'Why don't you ser ... make sandwiches.' He swiftly changed his answer after glancing up to meet Fran's teasing smile. 'Ham, turkey and roasted vegetable. Half a dozen of each.'

'No probs.' The boy disappeared, whistling as he pushed open the kitchen door.

Charlie sized up Fran and bit back

the compliment hovering on the tip of his tongue. The beauty he'd recognised in her that first day was more apparent now, but he suspected she might not appreciate the compliment. 'Survived your first morning?' A flash of heat coloured her neck. 'Patrick told me about your new job. That'll be great for Lucy.'

'We're working together today, but tomorrow could be a baptism of fire.'

'I'm sure you'll cope. What can I get for you anyway?' he asked. 'I don't mean to be rude, but we're bound to be interrupted by more customers any minute now.'

'That's a good thing, right?'

'The interruption or the business?' He wanted to kick himself for the quasi-flirtatious question. Without quite meeting his gaze, Fran recited Lucy's order. 'What about you?'

'Me?'

'Yes. You do eat lunch, I assume?'

'Of course.' Fran scrutinised the menu board and the display case.

'Everything looks great. Surprise me. I'll leave my lunch completely in your hands.'

Her playful challenge surprised him. 'You might regret it.'

'Oh, I don't think so.'

If Charlie didn't know better, he'd think *he* was the one being flirted with.

'I see you've got cook books for sale.' She pointed towards the small selection he'd brought in. 'I love reading them.'

'And cooking?'

'Not so much,' she said with a laugh, and wandered away.

Charlie got busy with her order, doing Lucy's first before deciding what to make for Fran. After nearly twenty years in the food business, he could usually guess a customer's menu choice on the spot. If he got it wrong, it was normally because they'd ordered something other than what they really wanted. He smiled to himself as he filled up the distinctive blue and white checked box, quickly snapping it closed so she wouldn't be able to see inside.

'Aren't you a dark horse!' Fran held up a book. 'Lucy told me you had a restaurant in London before this, but she didn't say you were a celebrity.'

'Don't talk rot,' he scoffed. 'It's a recipe book. That's all.'

She turned the book over, throwing him a mischievous smile as she began to read. 'Charming Charlie Boscawen reveals his culinary secrets. The chef/owner of the popular Cornish Chough restaurant shows us why he's beloved by thousands of fans, primarily of the female variety. They can't resist his — '

'Cut it out. They make up that stuff to sell books.'

Fran's bare-faced stare made his cheeks burn. 'I don't think so.'

'Hey, mate, give us a bag of scones and a couple of millionaire slices for Mum.'

Charlie had rarely been so glad to see a customer, even if it was Toby Watkins, the reviled local traffic warden who enjoyed his job far too much. 'Let me get this lady on her way first.' He totalled up Fran's order. 'That'll be fifteen pounds twenty. Unless you're buying the book as well?'

She met his smile with a broad one of her own. 'Not today. But I'll definitely think about it.' Fran passed over the money and the tips of their fingers brushed together, sending a zing of awareness through Charlie.

'Good,' he said, and gave her a wink before lowering his voice to a whisper. 'That was the general idea.' He handed her the picnic box. 'Enjoy.'

'I'm sure I will. I'll let you know my opinion,' she laughingly promised.

Charlie went back to work, his go-to way of solving problems. And if Francesca Miller wasn't one, then he would eat his chef's hat.

6

'What's the verdict after your first week?' Lucy asked the moment Fran walked in the door on Friday.

All she wanted to do was collapse in a hot bath and go straight to bed, but her friend was eager to talk. 'I've got to say I admire you so much more now,' she declared, dropping into the nearest comfy chair. 'I can't believe I thought it would be easy. I suppose it's the fact that one minute you've got a child having a nosebleed over your desk, and next thing a tourist pops in asking where to buy the best ice cream.'

Lucy laughed so hard she could hardly catch her breath. 'That's the funniest thing I've heard in ages.'

'Thanks. I'm glad I'm good for something, even if it's only amusing you,' she pretended to complain. 'Truthfully, I love it.'

'Really?'

'Yeah, really. I'm grateful to Patrick for being fussy and to you for giving in to him.'

'He had a point.' Lucy's smile faded. 'You know it's been a struggle for us to get to this point, and . . . I won't do anything to risk this precious baby.'

Fran nodded, her throat too constricted to speak. Her friends had been married for nearly ten years and had almost given up hope of having the family they longed for. She understood that sentiment far more than they realised. She reached over and touched Lucy's hand. 'You're helping me as well.'

'Are you ready to tell me what happened?' Lucy asked.

'I don't think so.' Fran tried to soften her refusal. 'I'm getting closer though, so that's encouraging.' She wasn't sure how true that was, but it eased the strain on her friend's face. Sometimes a white lie was the best solution. *Keep telling yourself that.*

'Good. By the way, do you have any plans this evening?'

The sudden sparkle of mischief in Lucy's eyes threw up instant red flags. 'Apart from a long soak in the bath?'

'Yes, apart from that, oh boring friend.'

Fran reluctantly admitted she didn't.

'Perfect. Patrick's bullied Charlie into coming here for dinner tonight.'

'Did he need bullying? I would think he'd be glad not to have to cook after doing it all day.'

Lucy shrugged. 'He feels obliged to see to his parents, even though to be honest his mother's perfectly capable, and I've heard her tell him so many times. His dad's an old misery. I know he's not very well, but George Boscawen's always been a hard man from what I've heard around the village.'

'By the way, I've got a bone to pick with you,' Fran complained. 'I meant to tell you on Monday when I got back from picking up our lunch. Why didn't you tell me Charlie was famous?' She explained about the cookbook and his embarrassed reaction.

'He plays it down these days, and I'm surprised he's even selling them in the shop.' Lucy gave her a long hard stare. 'You're not totally unknown yourself, and I haven't heard you mention a word about that since you've been here.'

'Okay, I get the hint.'

'Charlie said he'd be here around sixish, if you want to freshen up before he arrives. Patrick should be home by then too. We'll eat at seven.'

'Can I do anything to help?'

Lucy grinned. 'Wear a dress.'

'You're not match-making, remember?'

'Cross my heart and hope to die. It never occurred to me.'

'Right. That poor baby's going to have a liar for a mother,' she retorted. As she hurried from the room, her friend's unladylike language followed close behind.

Flowers? Wine? Cookies? Charlie ran over the possibilities. On the rare times he'd eaten with Patrick and Lucy, he'd grabbed a bottle of inexpensive wine on the way to their house. But with Lucy being pregnant, that wasn't an option. Cookies might be seen as leftovers that hadn't sold today, and flowers struck him as a cop-out, the refuge of the unadventurous.

Chocolate. You could never go wrong with chocolate where women were concerned. He locked up the shop and headed straight for Kernow Choklet. His friend, Anna Tremayne, made the most amazing chocolates he'd ever tasted. Ten minutes later he emerged with her largest box, a selection of plain, milk and white to cover all possible tastes. As a bit of a culinary pedant, he objected to the use of the word 'chocolate' where the white variety was concerned. Strictly speaking, it shouldn't be labelled chocolate because it didn't contain cacao mass, the ground beans; only cocoa butter.

Don't be such an old woman. This was what living with his father too long was doing to him.

He'd left Robbie in charge and run home in the middle of the afternoon when things were quiet to take his parents a bacon and egg pie for their tea, along with a bowl of salad and a strawberry trifle. His father would still complain later, but Charlie didn't care.

Along by the harbour wall, he stopped for a few minutes to gaze out over the sea. Today it was a dark vibrant green, reminding him of fresh basil and Fran's sparkling eyes. He chuckled to himself. She might not appreciate being compared to a herb, but from his viewpoint that was a compliment. He kept going and soon found himself in Pydar Street outside the Hunts' attractive house, made from local Cornish granite and weathered to a muted soft grey and cream. When he'd bought his own house, he'd be on the lookout for something similar. He'd been resentful when he moved back to Tresidder, but as the weeks slipped by the idea of staying permanently was growing on him.

He rubbed a smudge of flour off the right leg of his jeans. It was too late now, but he wished he'd taken the time to shower and change after his long day at work.

'Are you going to stand there all day, or come in and join us?' Patrick appeared in the front door, waving two bottles of Tribute beer in the air. 'Will this help to make up your mind?'

Charlie ambled up the path. 'Maybe.' He grabbed the bottle and laughed. 'Cheers.' He popped off the top and took a long drink, the rich hoppy flavours hitting all the right taste buds.

'Charming.' Lucy appeared, looking disgusted. 'Are you two going to stand on the doorstep drinking like a couple of teenagers sneaking around behind their parents' backs?'

'Never get married, mate. All they do

is nag.' The broad smile plastered all over his face mitigated Patrick's complaint.

'You look hard done by.' Truthfully, he envied his friend. He'd had plans in the same direction once, but they'd been scuppered by Alex's death. Burying herself in the wilds of Cornwall to help Charlie to run an upmarket sandwich shop hadn't been Melissa's idea of a sparkling future. She'd had no qualms in dumping him and latching onto one of his more successful friends. Though that might be unfair of him, because Melissa's reasons hadn't been all selfish. Time had blunted the initial hurt, and now he could barely remember what'd drawn them together in the first place.

'Fran and I are going out to the back garden with some nibbles to tide us over until dinner's ready,' Lucy announced.

'Will these help to stave off the hunger pangs?' He thrust the chocolates at her.

'OMG. You've been to Anna's.' She snatched the box from his hands and kissed his cheek. 'If I wasn't already married, I'd snatch you up.' Lucy glared at Patrick. 'And don't you dare to say they're bad for me or I'll stab you through the heart.'

'Wouldn't dare.' Patrick threw up his hands.

'Five minutes. Be there,' she warned, and stepped back into the house.

'You heard the boss.'

'Hang on a sec,' Charlie pleaded. 'I haven't had a chance to ask if you told Fran about that man.'

'What man?' Fran suddenly appeared, and her crisp tone cut through his question. 'Come on, who's going to tell — '

'He will.' Patrick pointed at Charlie. 'I'm going to take care of my bride.'

'I'm surprised smoke didn't come out of his heels,' she snapped. 'Well? I'm waiting.'

'Last Saturday an American came in as I was getting ready to close up the shop.' He watched her closely. 'Said his name was Randy Seacrest.'

Fran's whole body tensed. 'Did he ask for me by name?'

'Yeah, he claimed to be an old friend.'

'What made you guess he was talking about me?' she persisted.

'Your accent isn't a dead giveaway, but he showed me a photo, and although you've obviously changed your hair, it was unmistakeably you.'

'The accent rubs off. I was born in Plymouth and moved around a lot growing up because my father was in the navy, but I've lived in California since I left uni.' Fran couldn't quite look at him. 'The . . . situation with Randy is difficult to explain.'

'In case you're worried, I didn't tell Seacrest I recognised you.'

'Thanks. Will you let me know if he comes around again?'

'Of course,' he promised. 'How about we go in and put our hosts' minds at rest?' She threw him a questioning look.

'They're probably worried that you've ripped me to shreds by now.'

'If I know Lucy, she'll have decided that you've succeeded in wooing me and swept me into a romantic embrace by this time.'

'Was that an offer?' Charlie teased.

'Certainly not,' she retorted before giving in to a bubble of laughter.

'We'll see.' He gestured for Fran to go in first and she frowned, obviously suspicious, as if he was up to something. Which he absolutely was.

7

Fran eyed the hired bicycle with trepidation.

'You'll love it. It's a gorgeous day and there aren't too many visitors around yet.' Charlie's attempt at reassurance landed on deaf ears. The last time she'd ridden, Fran was fifteen, and she'd fallen off and ripped her knee open on rough gravel. Naturally last night Lucy and Patrick had encouraged her when Charlie suggested the two of them tackled the Pentewan Cycle Trail.

It's a gentle ride along by the St. Austell River, and there are a lot of decent paved tracks and shady woods to ride through. We'll hardly be on the roads at all.

At eight o'clock this morning, Fran began to have second thoughts when her alarm went off, followed rapidly by third and fourth ones. Apart from the whole bicycle thing, spending time alone with Charlie was a terrible idea. The problem was that his simple kindness and sense of fun last night had drawn her in and made it impossible to say no.

'I'll treat you to some excellent roast beef at the Ship Inn when we're done,' he promised. 'Do you trust my food instincts after the lunch I chose for you the other day?'

'I suppose so. How did you guess what I'd like anyway?' He'd got her exactly right with healthy roasted vegetables in whole-wheat pita bread, a bottle of sparkling water, and a couple of sinful dark chocolate and cherry cookies to round it all off.

'I've been in the business a long time,' he said with a shrug.

'Not sure I like being predictable.'

Charlie opened his mouth to speak but closed it again.

'Let's get on with this ride,' Fran sighed.

His vibrant blue eyes pierced through

her and she fought against blushing.

'Your dark eyelashes are totally not right for a fair-haired man,' she mused.

'Are you accusing me of wearing mascara or fake lashes?' A warm smile blossomed over his whole face deepening the attractive creases around his eyes. She'd worked out that Charlie must be a few years older than her but he wore his age lightly. In khaki shorts and a loose white T-shirt, his sun-streaked hair caught in the gentle breeze, and the light caught the soft stubble on his unshaven jaw.

'I sure hope not.'

'They're inherited from my mother. My brother's were the same.' The tight smile didn't reach his eyes. 'Being identical twins, they would be.'

'It must be like losing half of yourself,' she ventured.

'Yes, but it's worse in some ways because we weren't good friends when he died. We'd had our differences.'

'I'm sure he knew deep down that you loved him.'

'I hope so,' he murmured. 'I know he loved me.'

'Because he took on the shop when you didn't want to?' Fran guessed.

'Yes. It's a long story.'

'Maybe you'd better save it for another day.'

'Good plan.' Charlie lowered his mouth towards hers but turned at the last second to brush her cheek with his warm, firm lips. 'I could get to like you.'

'I already like you,' she murmured, 'far more than I should.'

'Ditto.' He cracked another tantalising smile. 'I was simply trying to be polite.'

'I suspect we're a bit past that, don't you?'

'Are you calling me old?'

'Of course not.' Fran grinned. 'Would you like me to get on my bike? In more ways than one perhaps?'

'I can't believe I've found a woman whose sense of humour matches mine. Of course, that's been called warped at times, so you might not consider it a compliment.'

'Oh, Charlie, thank you.'

'What for, love?' The familiar Cornish endearment, used by everyone from supermarket cashiers to bus drivers, sounded more intimate coming from him.

'Reminding me it's okay to laugh even if everything in our lives isn't perfect.'

'That's when we need it most,' he whispered and cradled her hands. The gentle touch sent a shimmer of longing surging through Fran. 'Time for our bike ride, I think.'

The spell broke.

★   ★   ★

Cycling was good when a person didn't want to talk, and Charlie hoped Fran would become more at ease around him today.

'We're doing the straightforward loop minus the extra ride up to the Eden

Project or to Heligan Gardens. We'll save the more strenuous stuff for another day.'

Fran's eyebrows rose. 'You think there'll be one?'

'I hope so.' Charlie left it there and a rush of heat zoomed up to flood her face. 'Follow me.' Without another word, he led the way from the car park over to the trail. 'Shout if you have any problems or want to stop.' He hadn't taken his bike out in ages and soon settled into an easy rhythm, enjoying the fresh air after being stuck indoors all week. Occasionally he glanced over his shoulder to check on Fran, and when she wasn't concentrating hard on cycling he received a few smiles in return. The trail wended its way along the riverbank before dipping back in through woodland and emerging again into the sunshine.

'We'll be going along the road for a little while up here.' He gestured ahead of them. 'Traffic's not bad today, but be careful.' A slight frown crossed Fran's face. 'Hey, don't worry, I'll take care of you.' He checked for traffic and crossed the narrow road before turning into a quiet lane. 'We'll turn around at the end of this.'

'Already?'

He grinned. 'Too soon?'

Fran shook her head. 'I suspect I'll be sore tomorrow, but I don't mind admitting I'm enjoying this more than I expected.'

'Maybe it's the company?' Again a tinge of colour caught her cheekbones, and for a second Charlie was blindsided by her beauty. Even with no make-up and wearing a bicycle helmet, Fran was stunning.

'I suspect it's the lure of roast beef and Yorkshire puddings. I haven't had that in years,' she neatly circumvented his teasing question.

They reached the end of the pleasantly shaded lane and Charlie stopped, leaning half on and half off his bike. 'I'm getting a drink before we head back.'

'Good idea.' Fran wobbled to a halt and he made a grab for her arm to steady her. He reached down and tugged her water bottle out of its clasp. 'Thanks.'

A contented silence fell between them as they drank, broken only by birdsong and the faint hum of traffic in the distance.

'That's better.' Charlie wiped his mouth and wished he had the courage to say something more profound, dig a little underneath the surface of Fran's protective mask. But if he did, she might turn the tables on him and demand the same in return. 'Ready for lunch?' For one brief moment, he could've sworn a flash of disappointment skittered across her face.

'Always.'

'I'll give you a gentle push to get you going again and then pull out ahead to lead the way. Okay?'

'I guess so.'

'You're doing great,' he tried to encourage her. Plainly she'd been metaphorically knocked down and was struggling to get back up again. If anyone knew how that felt, it was Charlie.

They set off, and the return ride seemed to go faster. Before they knew it, they were back outside the cycle hire shop and had returned Fran's bicycle. Charlie tossed his helmet into the back of his delivery van before loading his bicycle and giving his messed-up hair a quick run-through with his fingers. 'This is as good as it's going to get, I'm afraid.'

'Don't worry. We're not out to impress each other . . . are we?' A thread of apprehension sneaked through Fran's voice.

'Of course not,' Charlie lied through clenched teeth. 'We'll leave the van here and walk. It's not far.'

Fran's smile returned. 'Let's see if my legs still work.'

The instant response trickled through his mind that her long tanned legs looked extremely good from where he was standing. She'd worn shorts today too, and teamed them with a pretty yellow T-shirt. Apart from their almost-kissing moment earlier, she'd made it clear that he wasn't what she needed right now.

'Roast beef and Yorkshire puddings, here we come.' He'd got the science of light flirtation off perfectly. Fran never needed to know she'd made him rethink everything.

8

'How did yesterday's cycling date go with our charming baker?'

Lucy's eagerness embarrassed Fran. 'It wasn't a date,' she muttered.

'Right. Pull the other one, it's got bells on. Two single people who're obviously attracted to each other go out together — do they call that something different in America?'

'The bike ride was cool. It's a beautiful area,' Fran avoided answering. 'The pub lunch was delicious and I ate far too much. Charlie's good company. End of story.'

Lucy snorted. 'It's all you're telling me, but I know you too well, Francesca Miller.'

'No, you knew the younger version of me, but I've grown up the same as you. I'm not interested in a relationship with any man at the moment, no matter how good-looking and tempting he might be.'

'Aha, I knew you fancied him.'

'It'd be hard not to,' Fran said with a sigh. 'We both know all the women around here swoon over Charlie. You admitted it yourself. *You* don't do anything about it because you're happily married. *I'm* not doing anything about it because . . . '

'I'm waiting.' The tough edge to Lucy's voice threw her back to their days at university when her friend would grill her relentlessly after a night out, demanding every detail and not giving in until satisfied. Fran had avoided the inquisition yesterday because Patrick and Lucy had gone to visit his parents in Exeter and didn't get home until after she'd already gone to bed. 'Who's Randy Seacrest?'

The sudden change of topic threw her for a loop.

'Do I have to drag it out of you?' Lucy persisted.

'Do you annoy your poor husband

this way? You're like a dripping tap.'

Her friend positively smirked.

'Fine,' Fran conceded, and took a seat at the kitchen table across from Lucy. 'Randy's my agent and we were . . . involved personally, but not anymore. He doesn't know I'm here.' She quickly corrected herself. 'At least, he's not supposed to.'

'Why not?' Lucy leaned across and got right in her face.

'Leave it alone. Please.'

'Sorry. Patrick always says I never know when to stop.'

'I appreciate you wanting to help. Honestly.' She grabbed her friend's hands and held on tight. There were few people she'd ever completely trusted, and the woman sitting in front of her was one of them. Fran suspected Charlie could be another, but dare not get close enough to find out.

'Let me,' Lucy whispered.

Fran shook her head and couldn't meet her friend's sympathetic gaze. 'I can't.' She jumped back up. 'That's enough moping for one day. If it's all right with you, I'm off to have a long hot shower to get my joints moving. My ogre of a boss will be cross if I'm late for work or need an appointment myself to get my sore knees seen to.'

'You know very well Patrick's a big softie, but off you go.' She shooed her away. 'By the way, when are you seeing Charlie again?'

The glitter of amusement lurking in Lucy's eyes meant Fran couldn't get cross. 'Probably the next time I'm in his shop to buy food for my perennially starving hostess.' She held up her hand. 'And don't get the idea to send me there every day to scratch your matchmaking itch.'

'You are so boring these days,' Lucy groused.

'Yep, that's me, old and boring.'

'Who are you calling old? We're the same age,' she protested. 'It's bad enough to see primagravida written on my medical notes because I'm a first time mother who happens to be barely over thirty-five.'

Fran chuckled. 'Shower,' she blithely announced, and hurried off before Lucy could start on her again.

* * *

Charlie popped the envelope in the post box before he changed his mind. If Chantelle accepted his offer to visit her in France, he wasn't sure how he'd manage to keep the shop open, but inviting her to Cornwall wasn't an option.

He strolled along the quay, but didn't enjoy his solitary early morning walk as much as usual. The rising sun bathed the sky with a pale glow, gilding the dark calm water all the way to the horizon. He turned away and headed around the corner to his shop, still unable to get Fran out of his head.

When they'd got back to Tresidder yesterday, he'd taken Fran straight home, but neither of them had rushed to get out of the van. Foolishly, he'd leaned over and touched the side of her face, brushing his fingers along her soft velvety skin. Very foolishly, she'd let him.

'*I'd better go.*'

'*Do you want to?*'

'*No. But I must.*'

The whisper of her breath had shivered through him, but he'd nodded his agreement. Understanding only too well about things that had to be done, he'd let her go without another word.

Charlie walked into the shop and stopped in his tracks. He could have sworn he'd set all the chairs straight on Saturday before he left, but one was out of place. Glancing towards the chill cabinet, he automatically counted the number of drinks and discovered two bottles of lemonade were missing.

He made his way around to the till, but that was as he'd left it. Out in the back room, Charlie frowned down at the floor. The last thing he'd done was sweep thoroughly, but now there was a large floury footprint over by the back door. He stuck his head out and peered down the narrow alley running along behind the row of buildings, but there was nothing to be seen apart from the overflowing bins waiting to be emptied.

'Hey, Mr. B, how's it goin'?' Robbie sauntered in and headed towards the sink to wash his hands. 'Something up?'

'No, just me being daft.' Obviously he hadn't done as good a job of tidying up and restocking before he left as he'd thought, probably too keen to see Fran again. 'You have a good day off?'

The boy's thin face darkened.

'Is everything okay at home?' Charlie asked. Robbie's father had abandoned his family years ago, and his mother was a proud hard-working woman who struggled to keep her five children fed and clothed.

Robbie shrugged and opened the fridge.

'If you're hungry, fix something before we start.'

'I don't need your charity,' he snapped.

'I didn't mean it that way.'

'Yeah, whatever.' Robbie grabbed a baked ham and took it over to the slicer.

Charlie nodded and left the boy to it, turning his ovens on and getting ready to start his baking for the day. The quiches were first on his list, and he took out the cold butter from the fridge ready to make pastry. It would need to chill for at least an hour, and he'd use the waiting time to start on today's cakes.

I don't bite. Unless it's one of your Swiss rolls.

At a guess, he'd say Fran would love his alluring apricot recipe, a delicate almond sponge studded with diced fresh apricots, rolled with a soft almond-flavoured cream and home-made apricot purée. If she didn't come in today, he could justify delivering one to the house later by saying it was for Lucy. He smiled as an idea struck him.

He and Robbie worked hard for a couple of hours, only talking if it was necessary. The teenager had proved to be a hard worker from the day Charlie had taken him on, contrary to his school reports and the fact he'd left at sixteen with no qualifications. His manners were a bit rough around the edges, but he was learning fast. Several times recently, Charlie had noticed the boy's interest when he was baking and encouraged him to help out.

'Time for a break.' Charlie always tried to give them both a rest for a few minutes. He poured out two mugs of steaming hot coffee and set one down in front of Robbie. 'Try a scone with it and give me your opinion.'

Robbie eyed the plate suspiciously.

'I only made a small batch. It's a new recipe I'm trying out — not charity.' Maybe he shouldn't have said that, but Charlie was tired of everyone assuming they could guess his motives for doing things.

'What's in them?'

'You tell me.' Charlie smiled. 'Then I'll know if I got it right. Be honest about whether or not you like them.'

'You sure?'

'Of course. That's the only way a chef can improve.' Charlie took a swig of his coffee. 'Honesty works for most things in life.' Robbie's dark eyes fixed on him. 'Don't you agree?'

'I guess,' he mumbled, cramming a scone into his mouth.

Charlie wished he could find out what was going on with the kid.

'That's not bad.'

'Not bad?'

'It's got that funky cheese in, hasn't it? That Greek stuff. I'm not a fan.' Robbie quirked a smile. 'I like the oregano and touch of honey. Did you use Greek yogurt in there too?'

Charlie's jaw dropped. 'Seriously? You can taste all that?'

'Did I get it wrong?'

'No, you're spot on. You've got great tastebuds. That's something no one can teach.' He took a chance. 'Have you ever thought about doing a culinary course?' Robbie stared as if he was a madman. 'I know you didn't get on great in school, but this would be different, and I could help you.'

'I've got work to do.' He shoved the stool back out of the way and abandoned it where it was.

Charlie couldn't help remembering the out-of-place chair.

9

In the past, she'd been wooed with bouquets of exotic flowers, wined and dined at five-star restaurants, and memorably been taken once on a private jet to the opera in Milan — but never before with cake.

Fran hadn't seen Charlie since Sunday, but he'd made certain she didn't forget him. He'd been cunning and delivered freshly baked treats to Lucy every lunchtime while Fran was working. Alluring apricot Swiss roll on Monday. Sock it to me strawberry scones on Tuesday. Eager beaver éclairs on Wednesday. Luscious lips lemon cupcakes on Thursday. The corny names made them all roll their eyes, but now it was nearly six o'clock on Friday and she found herself dying to find out what today's cake would be.

'Ready to pack up?' Patrick stood by

her desk and yawned. 'Don't know about you, but I'm ready for the weekend.'

Fran knew enough of his work schedule now to understand he wouldn't have the next forty-eight hours completely free. For a start, he was on call until eight o'clock tonight, and then he'd use a portion of his time off to catch up on the mountains of paperwork that continued to accumulate. 'Have you got anything exciting planned?'

'Apart from sleep?' Patrick laughed and patted his stomach. 'I ought to do some exercise. I used to get up an hour early to run, but that's fallen by the wayside.' He cracked a sly smile. 'Of course, all the delicious cakes appearing in our house at regular intervals aren't helping.'

Fran's cheeks burned.

'You going to put the poor chap out of his misery before we all explode?'

To outsiders they might seem an ideal match, but she knew better and wasn't about to explain. Still, the memory of Charlie's fleeting touch wouldn't leave her alone.

'*I'd better go.*'

'*Do you want to?*'

'*No. But I must.*'

Charlie had seemingly accepted her reluctance, so why all the cakes? It didn't make sense. But whoever said love made sense, Fran reprimanded herself. He fancied her — that was all.

Patrick touched her shoulder. 'Sorry. Put my big feet in it again. Lucy says I'm an insensitive beast.'

'Yeah, well, you're a man,' Fran quipped. 'Don't fret. I'm not going to shatter into a thousand pieces because of a bit of teasing.'

'Good.'

'Let's hurry home and see what goodies arrived today.'

'Sounds like a plan.'

She could've kissed him for playing along with her. She gathered her things together and stepped outside to wait on Patrick while he locked up. They set off down the hill, and by unspoken agreement walked along quietly, savouring the lingering sunshine mixed with a hint of salt-laden breeze whipping up around from the harbour.

'There's nowhere quite like Cornwall for beautiful summer evenings,' she mused. 'It's got a softness that's missing in California.'

'You'll go back?'

'I'm not sure.' Fran shrugged. 'Apart from my dad and a few friends, I don't have many ties, and I can write anywhere. At least, I usually can. If I could only come up with an idea for my next book, it'd help.' She tossed out the nugget of truth without thinking and caught Patrick's quizzical glance. 'When I spoke to my father, he said he's considering an offer from the aquarium in Plymouth,' she rushed on. 'It would be an easier job, and the change of scenery might do him good.'

When they stopped outside the house, she glanced at Patrick. 'No wonder your patients say you're easy to talk to.' She'd blurted out far more than she'd intended, and in another few minutes who knew what other secrets she'd have spilled.

'Don't worry, I never repeat anything I'm told,' he assured her. 'Not even to Lucy.' Patrick grinned. 'Especially not to Lucy. You know I worship the ground she walks on, but she does love to gossip.' A shadow crossed his face. 'The biggest row we've ever had was because she repeated something she heard at the surgery to one of her friends. It caused some trouble and I had to smooth things over.'

Fran appreciated the subtle warning. Of course she knew her old friend wasn't always the most discreet person, but there was a lot more at stake now than when they were schoolgirls.

'Let's go in and see what waistline-destroyers we've got tonight!' He laughed and pushed open the gate, standing back to let Fran go first.

I'm more concerned about heart destroyers — and not the medical sort.

★ ★ ★

Time to make a personal delivery. Charlie smoothed down his hair and rubbed his fingers over his freshly shaved jaw to check he hadn't missed any spots. The miniature frangipane tartlets he'd made were spectacular. He'd tweaked the classic French recipe and used hazelnuts instead of almonds in the pastry cream and studded them with plump raspberries. He finished tying silver and green ribbons around the box. 'I'm off.'

'Making a fool of yourself over that woman, I suppose?' His father's snide question stopped Charlie with his hand on the door. How did a man who rarely left the house keep such close tabs on what was happening in the village? He'd purposely not mentioned Fran, instead referring vaguely to 'a friend' when they'd gone cycling together.

'What does some fancy writer want with you?'

'Writer?'

'Didn't you know?' George sniggered. 'Oh, that's a good one.'

'Go on. I can tell you're itching to.'

'Charlie, that's unkind,' his mother complained. He resisted the temptation to reply that 'kind' was the last word he'd use to describe his father.

'F. E. Miller. The Calendar Corpses mystery series. I'm halfway through the latest one.' He picked up a book from the coffee table and shoved it towards Charlie. 'Be careful she doesn't put you in her next book,' he snorted.

Taking it out of his father's hand, he examined the garish front cover with its embossed silver lettering and shadowy figure holding an ornate dagger dripping with blood. *Ordeal in October*. Charlie flipped it open and checked out the author information. The glamorous picture was the exact same one Randy Seacrest had shown him.

'They used to keep it quiet about F. E. Miller being a woman, but when the books got popular I suppose it didn't matter.' He shrugged. 'She's good.'

'How did you — '

'Put two and two together?' His father's eyes narrowed. 'I'm not daft. Harry Winston popped in to see me a few days ago and mentioned meeting the new receptionist up at the surgery. He told me her name and said she had a bit of an American accent. I showed him the book, and he was fairly certain it was the same woman.' George smirked. 'Then Harry was watering his garden Sunday afternoon and spotted her getting out of your van.'

'And I suppose he couldn't resist ringing up to tell you?' Charlie retorted.

'So what?'

He shouldn't complain. This was village life, and if he didn't like it he should clear off back to London where you could live next to someone for twenty years and never know their name. Charlie wished Fran had trusted him enough to mention what she did for a living. He didn't care about the well-known part, because he'd dipped his toe in that pond himself and didn't care for the temperature of the water. When he'd probed while they ate their Sunday lunch, she'd neatly evaded his questions and muttered something vague about being 'in advertising' back in California.

'Trying to win her over with your cakes, are you?' His father chuckled, but there was no hint of good humour in his hard slate-grey eyes. 'Waste of bloody time, if you ask me. She — '

'I didn't ask you,' Charlie snapped. 'See you later, Mum.' He hated the tension creased deep in her face, making her look far older than sixty. Losing Alex had knocked all the stuffing out of her. She'd always been quiet, but had become so withdrawn it worried him.

'Have a good time,' she ventured, throwing his father an apologetic smile.

'I'm only popping over to see the Hunts.' He didn't add that he'd be back pretty quickly if Fran turned him down.

He'd given his unusual wooing strategy a shot this week because he'd spotted his own longing and regret reflected back in her gaze when they parted on Sunday. Maybe he'd made a huge mistake. He plainly knew nothing about Fran, at least far less than he'd thought. Should he ask her about F. E. Miller, or wait for her to reveal things in her own time? Charlie hadn't got a clue.

Clasping the cake box, he left the house and prepared to win over the most interesting woman he'd met in years with his frangipane tarts.

You plonker. Alex's ribald laughter echoed in the air as clearly as if he'd been standing next to Charlie.

Stuff it.

Only teasing you. Go for it, mate.

Charlie grinned and turned the corner into Pydar Street. If it didn't sound crazy, he'd say Alex had forgiven him.

10

Fran felt the weight of Charlie's scrutiny as she opened the lid of the box. He wasn't the only one watching because Lucy and Patrick were squeezed on either side of her at the front door.

'I thought you'd forgotten us today, mate,' Patrick joked. 'The girls were disappointed.' He tapped Fran's shoulder. 'Particularly this one.'

Her cheeks burned with embarrassment, but she kept staring at the most exquisite mini-tartlets she'd ever seen outside of a French bakery. It was hard to believe Charlie's big hands could've fashioned something so tiny and perfect. But that wasn't what swept away her ability to speak. On the top of each tart, he'd etched a letter in delicate pale pink icing and formed them into words.

Dinner tomorrow night? Yes I'm

trying to impress you and yes this is a date.

An even fiercer blush heated her body all the way down to her toes as she met Charlie's searing gaze.

'Of course she will, where — '

'Lucy, zip it,' Patrick remonstrated. 'We'll leave you two to talk.'

'But — '

'But nothing. Get your cute little self back inside and put your feet up. Doctor's orders.'

Fran suppressed a laugh as her friend pouted and allowed herself to be steered back into the living room. Patrick closed the door behind them and she breathed properly again.

'Are you going to put me out of my misery?' Charlie murmured.

'What are they called?'

'Huh?'

'These tart things. You've given everything else crazy names all week. Don't tell me they're simply tarts.'

He quirked one eyebrow. 'Crazy names? I'll have you know I plan out

94

my marketing strategy very carefully.'

'Oh come on, Cake Romeo, you can do better than 'tart'.' Fran's use of Patrick's teasing name for her errant baker earned her a half-hearted glare. 'Alluring apricot, sock it to me, eager beaver and luscious lips. You've a lot to live up to today.'

'The ones I made for the shop were freakin' Friday frangipanes.'

'But?'

He fixed her with what she suspected Edna Kittow would call a vintage Paul Hollywood stare. 'These are a special batch I made for you. They're fabulous Francesca frangipanes.' Charlie carefully took away the box and placed it on the floor before clasping her hands. The imprint of his warm, strong fingers on her skin soothed Fran's ruffled nerves. 'The tarts say what I couldn't on Sunday. I lied. I've wanted to impress you from the day we met.'

'Why?' she croaked.

'You're beautiful. You interest me. You make me laugh.' He rested a hand lightly over her heart. 'Plus I really, really want to know what's in here. One date. Give me a chance.'

Fran's resolve to turn him down wavered before shattering into a thousand pieces. 'All right, I'll come. If nothing else, it'll stop you bombarding us with cake.' Her attempt to make light of his offer made a wide, beautiful smile light up his face. Anyone would think she'd given him a million pounds. 'I suspect you're in for a major disappointment. I'm not that fascinating.'

'We'll see.' Very cleverly, he didn't argue.

'Do you want to come in for a while?' Fran gestured over her shoulder. 'I'm sure Lucy's ready to explode with curiosity by now and dying to get her hands on your tarts,' she joked.

'I wouldn't want to be responsible for a dear friend's untimely demise.' Charlie laughed and let go of her. He picked up the abandoned box. 'As Marie Antoinette said — let them eat cake.'

'Have a good evening, Mr. B.' Robbie said with a cheeky wink. 'Don't do anything I wouldn't do!' He'd gotten great mileage out of Charlie's upcoming date with Fran and made fun of him all day.

'I'll try not to. Enjoy your day off.' The boy's smile faded and he wished he'd thought before speaking. 'Take care of yourself. Okay?'

'Sure. See ya Monday.'

Charlie let him go because in the end he was Robbie's employer, not a social worker. *Doesn't mean you can't care and get involved.* Alex used to berate him for standing back and observing rather than diving in and getting dirty where life was concerned. The last time he'd said it, they'd been arguing about Chantelle.

Marry her? Are you mad? She won't fit in here.

Are you afraid I'm going to chuck it

all in to go to France and stick you with this place?

Despite Charlie's quick apology, the damage had been done. He'd tried to convey his reservations because he couldn't see the sophisticated French-woman living in Tresidder, but Alex had homed in on Charlie's selfish tendencies.

He made his way methodically around the shop and checked that everything was in order before locking up. A rare lightness of spirit made him walk briskly along the quay, greeting people he knew but without stopping to get drawn into conversation. His usual Saturday evening routine consisted of a couple of hours in the Green Man beating Patrick at snooker or having a quiet drink on his own if his friend was busy. In the two years since he'd returned to Cornwall, this was his first proper date, although there weren't many people who'd believe that. He'd carefully crafted his reputation as a charming flirt who lived and breathed baking. Charlie had mentally prepared himself to work as many hours as necessary to get the business on a solid footing again before re-evaluating his personal life. That plan fell apart the moment Fran Miller walked through the door of Boscawen's Bites.

Charlie had thought long and hard about where to take Fran tonight because he wanted to strike the right note. Too fancy and it would scare her off; too ordinary and she wouldn't be impressed. He'd decided to take a chance that a California girl would be a beach lover and chosen one of his favourite spots, the Watering Hole in Perranporth. Set on three miles of golden sand, it had the UK's only bar on a beach, and the view at sunset was pretty much unmatched.

Back at the house, he intended to make the most of getting ready without his parents hovering around. Aunt Julie, his mother's sister, lived in Newquay, and she'd picked them up early this afternoon to go out for a drive. They planned to have a meal together later and wouldn't be back until after Charlie was long gone. He wasn't going to spoil the evening worrying about anything.

* * *

Several loud knocks on the front door stopped the quasi-argument Fran and Lucy were having about who was more handsome, Aidan Turner or James Norton. In her mind there was absolutely no doubt that the *Poldark* heartthrob won hands down.

'I'll let Charlie in.' Fran jumped up before Lucy could prise herself off the sofa.

'You look lovely. You're going to wow him.'

She wasn't sure that was her intention, but kept her uncertainty to herself. Charlie had been quite specific about what she should wear, and Fran hoped the loose-fitting green and gold Indian print dress, flat gold sandals and a delicate cream pashmina would fit the bill.

Something casual. Shoes suitable for walking on sand. A cardigan or wrap for if it gets cool.

Patrick and Lucy gave each other knowing smirks when she repeated Charlie's orders but refused to be drawn on where he might be planning to take her.

'Come in. If you don't — '

'Shush.' Charlie held up a warning finger. 'Let's sneak away. We're not teenagers and they're not our parents.' His eyes glittered with mischief and Fran couldn't help smiling back. She stepped outside and Charlie reached behind her to quietly close the door. They heard Lucy yelling out their names but ignored her and hurried out to the road.

'Oh, wow!' Fran ogled the gleaming sports car. 'My dad would drool over this beauty. I've never seen a 1964 TR4 with the correct signal-red paintwork before.'

'Don't tell me you're a classic car nut?'

She shrugged. 'By default. They've always been my dad's passion, but Mum wasn't interested, so I pretended to like them to spend more time with him. I guess they grew on me.'

'What does he drive?'

'His everyday ride is a Land Rover, but his pride and joy is a 1978 Triumph Spitfire he restored himself.'

'Very nice.' Charlie rested his warm hands on her waist. 'Rather like you.'

'Well-restored, you mean?' The effect of him standing so close made Fran's voice wobble. The evening sun picked up the gleam in his slightly too-long hair, curling over the collar of his crisp blue check shirt, and a subtle waft of expensive cologne teased her senses.

'If I say I meant that you and the car are both beautiful, will it scare you away?' A frown creased his forehead.

'I don't know. It might.' She struggled to be honest.

'I won't say it out loud again,' Charlie

promised, but the hint of a smile curved the edges of his mouth. 'At least not until I guess it might be safe to risk another try.'

'Are you a mind reader?' Fran wasn't sure if it bothered her that he'd known exactly what she was thinking.

'We'll find out, won't we?' He dropped his hands back to his sides and opened the passenger door. 'Are you ready for our mystery tour? I assume you like mysteries?' A subtle edge to his voice caught her off guard.

Her stomach churned. Somehow he knew about F. E. Miller. The question now was how to answer his inevitable questions.

11

Charlie strongly considered giving himself a swift kick up the backside. The last thing he'd intended was to spoil the evening before they even left Tresidder. What on earth had made him say such a dumb thing? The only pathetic excuse he could drag up was that he'd been knocked off balance by Fran's other-worldly beauty tonight. Her exotic dress brought out the warm glow of her honeyed skin and combined with the flash of Fran's vibrant green eyes to draw Charlie in.

'I — ' she began.

'Forget I spoke,' he pleaded.

'I can't.' She glanced anxiously back over her shoulder. 'Can we talk on the way?'

'Sure. I'm sorry.'

She brushed her fingers over his bare forearm where he'd rolled up his shirt sleeves, and the light touch set his pulse racing. 'Don't be. I should've been more honest with you.'

'Maybe, but I haven't exactly been Mr. Open either. I'm willing to try if you are.' He caught her hesitation and mentally crossed his fingers. 'Or we can simply have a pleasant evening and leave the confessions for another day.'

Fran tucked in her dress and hopped into the car, flashing a bright false smile up at him. 'Let's aim for both — we're adults. How hard can it be?'

Charlie didn't answer.

'Come on. Show me what she can do.' She patted the car and he couldn't resist the challenge. He eased into first gear and pulled away from the kerb. 'Oh my, she absolutely purrs.' Fran's eyes sparkled. 'Does she have a name?'

'Norma Jean,' Charlie murmured, and kept his gaze fixed on the road.

'Marilyn Monroe. Every man's dream woman. Can't go wrong with that,' she mused. 'My dad's is The Divine Etta J. He's a huge jazz fan.'

He didn't feel quite as stupid now. Fran was that rare woman who got his obsession with cars. 'Good one.' He headed out of Tresidder. 'Instead of driving straight there, we're taking a slightly longer route to see a beautiful part of the coast.'

'I'm not even going to ask where 'there' is,' Fran teased.

'Good. Wise move.' He clasped the wheel easily and settled back to enjoy the trip. There hadn't been enough of these moments recently, and he wanted to make the most of tonight. Norma Jean ran well considering she hadn't been driven in a while, and the weather couldn't be more perfect. He sneaked a quick peek at Fran, leaning back in the seat with her eyes closed. The wind whipped the strands of dark hair around her face, longer now than when they'd first met and slowly returning to its original brunette colour. After seeing her author picture with shoulder-length hair, he decided the new style suited her, revealing more of the elegant planes and hollows of her face.

'In twins the firstborn often becomes the leader, but that wasn't true in our case, and Alex never objected when I took charge,' Charlie dived in, hoping to take the burden off Fran. 'Dad made us help out in the bakery from the time we could see over the counter, and although Alex worked hard, he never enjoyed it.'

'I'm guessing you did?'

'Yep, couldn't get enough. But my dad and I always clashed, and I scraped through a few exams and chucked in school when I turned sixteen to work in the kitchen at the Green Man. Luckily 'Tiny' Williams took me under his wing and taught me everything he knew before packing me off to culinary school at eighteen.'

'I read your bio online,' Fran admitted.

'I worked for a lot of top chefs and opened my first restaurant at twenty-five.' Charlie tried to smile. 'I wasn't easy to work for, and I gave Gordon

Ramsay a run for his money in the bad-temper stakes.' He caught her surprise. 'I haven't always been charming, easygoing Charlie — not behind the scenes, anyway.'

'What did your family think?'

He pretended to concentrate on making his next turn while gathering his emotions. 'Dad's never had any patience with me.'

'Wasn't he proud of what you achieved? I saw you had two Michelin stars, and that's pretty awesome.'

Charlie shrugged. 'If he was, he never said so. He hammered on and on about me letting the family down by not taking over the shop.'

'I suppose Alex didn't really want to either?'

'No.' There was a lot more to the story, but Charlie couldn't manage it now.

'That's enough, I think.' Fran caught on to his mood yet again. 'Can mine wait until I've got a glass of wine in front of me?'

Her fake lightness didn't fool Charlie. His own carefully crafted image had become close to second nature until she'd come along and probed under the surface.

'Works for me, love. We'll be coming into Porthtowan in a minute.'

'Is that our destination for the evening?' she teased.

'Nope.'

'Makes perfect sense.'

'So it should,' Charlie said with a laugh. 'It's a pretty place, and we'll drive along the coast from there to St. Agnes and on to Perranporth, which is our final destination.' He draped his right hand over the side of the door. 'Norma enjoys a run along by the sea, don't you, pretty lady?'

'She doesn't have very good manners — she didn't answer you.'

'Oh she most certainly did,' he protested. 'Can't you hear the sweet sound of her engine ticking over perfectly? And don't roll your eyes at me, either.'

'Wouldn't dare. Now stop jabbering and let me enjoy the scenery.'

'Will do.' Charlie was happy to oblige. It meant no more difficult conversation and the chance to drink in the sight of Fran without her noticing. Both winning ideas.

Why she'd expected this to be a simple date, Fran couldn't imagine. Charlie was complex with a capital C. She'd fallen for easygoing flirtatious Charlie only because she'd sensed from that first day there was much more to him. What he'd told her so far didn't make for happy listening, but whose life did?

'You'll miss it all if you don't open your eyes,' he gently chided.

'Oops, sorry.' Fran kept to herself the fact that she thought better with her eyes closed, because it sounded borderline crazy. 'Wow, that's seriously gorgeous.' There were similarities to the more rugged parts of the California coastline along Highway 1, but Cornwall retained a uniqueness she couldn't pin down.

'Where do you think of as home?' he mused.

'Gee, that's a hard question. I've lived in California the longest of anywhere. How about you?'

'Do you really need to ask?' He sounded resigned. 'I wouldn't admit this to my dad, but I couldn't work in London again.' Charlie's fierce glare amused her. 'This place gets in your blood. Not sure there's any known cure.'

'Would you take it if there was?'

'No way.' Charlie fell silent again and kept driving. They slowly made their way through the charming village with its cluster of tiny cottages and seaside shops. 'When we crest this hill, you'll get one of the best views.'

'Will your other lady mind if we stop for a moment?'

'Not if I ask her nicely,' he quipped.

They pulled over into a narrow lay-by and Charlie turned off the engine, resting his large hands on the wheel. He angled his head to stare at her instead of the sea. 'Would you mind if I kissed you?'

'I'll mind a lot more if you don't,' she admitted, and Charlie's eyes darkened.

'Good.'

Unconsciously, Fran leaned towards him and he cradled her face with his palms, anchoring his fingers in her hair to pull her closer. She was hyper-aware of the play of his powerful muscles under the thin shirt. There was nothing tentative about his kiss, and her breathing raced out of control.

Charlie jerked away. 'And I thought Norma Jean was dangerous.' His attempt at humour failed, betrayed by the tremor threaded through his voice. Fran shared his shock at their instant connection, and the satisfied gleam in his eyes as they rested on her said he understood only too well.

'Maybe you should stop thinking and drive us to Perranporth — not that I've any idea what's there, but you obviously have a plan.'

'Oh, I do.' Charlie started up the

engine. 'I'm looking forward to my good-night kiss already.'

'You think you're going to get one?' She playfully jabbed his arm. 'It all depends on if you behave.'

A shadow settled around his mouth and drew it into a straight line. 'I'd never do anything — '

'I know that, silly man. I wouldn't be here otherwise. Come on, let's go and have some fun.'

'Excellent idea.'

She welcomed the roar of the engine coupled with the sharp breeze from the sea for their conversation-stopping qualities.

'We'll have to leave Norma Jean in one of the car parks and walk down to the beach,' Charlie explained.

'Hopefully you've got something in the way of food planned. Lunch is nothing but a distant memory, and I haven't had any amazing cakes today.' She managed a fake pout.

'Don't worry, you'll get fed, and there'll be another treat,' he promised, and proceeded to find a parking spot.

'You're like my dad. He always tucks his Triumph away from other cars, preferably into a corner.'

'I hope I'm not *too* like your father.' A devilish glint lit up his face. 'Let's go.' He hopped out and came around to open her door. 'Don't forget your shawl thing.'

'It's a pashmina. Old-fashioned grandmothers wear shawls.' Her attempt to sound offended failed when she giggled.

'Come on.'

They linked hands and set off walking, chatting happily as they went. Fran glanced at Charlie only to discover him smiling back at her.

'Feels right, doesn't it?'

She nodded, understanding exactly what he meant. Only after her relationship with Randy failed had Fran realised how uptight she'd been all the time they were together. That wasn't how it should be between two people supposedly in love. Could she really take another chance?

12

'Here we are, Perranporth beach,' Charlie said, steering her away from confusing thoughts about what might or might not be happening between them. He helped Fran down the last step onto the sand. 'We're in the middle of three miles of the best beaches in the whole of Cornwall.' He gestured over his right shoulder. 'That's Holywell,' he said, and then turned to point in the opposite direction. 'St. Agnes, where we drove by.'

'It's absolutely gorgeous.'

They kept on walking until a collection of low buildings came into view and the sound of people talking and laughing drifted across in the warm air.

'That's the Watering Hole. It's said to be the UK's only bar on a beach.

It's a restaurant and music and events venue too.'

'You knew where to bring me.' Fran beamed and bent down to slip off her sandals, swinging them in one hand and wiggling her toes. 'Warm sand under your feet. Nothing better.'

'I made a dinner reservation and assumed you'd prefer to sit outside.' Charlie showed her the rows of weathered tables and benches fronting the bar and restaurant.

'Definitely.' She gave him a hard stare. 'I'm guessing you're a sunset freak too?'

'Certainly am, and it's one of the best you'll ever see. Another thing we've got in common,' Charlie observed. 'I might have to marry you.' A brief slice of time hung between them before he laughed in an effort to convince her it was all a big joke.

'You're crazy.' Fran laughed too, and he made an effort to be grateful. 'Let's eat.'

Soon they were contentedly tucking

into huge portions of golden fish and chips.

'Somehow everything tastes better in the fresh air,' he said.

'Sure does.' She set down her knife and fork with an exaggerated sigh. 'I'm beaten.'

Charlie speared her remaining chips. 'Wimp.' He quickly ate them and pointed to her empty wine glass. 'Another? I'm sticking to water because of Norma Jean, but that doesn't have to stop you.'

'No, thanks. I made you a promise, didn't I?' Fran's small voice disturbed him and he slipped his arm around her.

'I don't want to spoil our first real date.' If he messed this up, there might not be a second. 'I never intended to put you on the spot tonight, only have fun together.'

'I put myself on it, didn't I? Be honest.' Fran leaned her head against his shoulder and strands of her silky hair brushed against his neck, sending a wisp of light floral scent his way. 'You'll think I'm loopy.'

He said nothing, and she haltingly began to talk. She gave him a potted history of her writing career, how it'd blossomed too fast and now she was suffering from a severe case of writer's block. With no ideas for book number eleven and a rapidly approaching deadline, she'd fled California. Fran joked about 'doing an Agatha Christie', but her face didn't light up.

'Losing my mother so suddenly made everything worse. We were close.' Fran closed her eyes as though she couldn't bear for him to see her pain. 'I used to bounce ideas off her all the time, and now . . . ' Her helpless shrug tugged at his heart.

'I suppose you've got to find a new way of working,' he ventured.

'Yeah, I know, but it's hard.'

Charlie stroked his hand over her hair, playing with the feathered ends. 'I'm a good listener.'

She glanced up, giving him a quirky

smile. 'You may wish you hadn't offered.'

'Never.'

'Never is a long time,' Fran warned.

'You'll miss it if you aren't careful.'

'What?'

Charlie nodded towards the horizon where a magical rosy light suffused the sky and flashes of gold and red picked out the tips of the waves. A strange quiet blanketed the beach as the chattering, laughing voices around them subsided to barely audible murmurs.

'Oh my.'

'Puts everything into perspective, doesn't it?' Charlie whispered, his breath warm on her skin.

Fran nodded through a glaze of tears.

'It'll do the same thing tomorrow and the day after . . . until it doesn't anymore.'

They didn't speak as the burning globe of light sunk into the sea, leaving behind a sprinkling of stars. Charlie's solid warmth surrounded her and she'd no desire to move.

'I think I'm falling in love with you, Fran.'

For a second she thought she'd misheard him, but he repeated the matter-of-fact statement.

'You know that's a terrible idea, don't you?'

'I can't seem to help it.'

'I don't know what to say,' Fran stumbled over her reply. The wariness she'd been forced to learn held her back from being more truthful.

'Are you ready to go home?' The resigned edge to Charlie's voice almost broke her resolve. 'Don't worry, I won't be stupid enough to say that again.'

She met his sad dark-eyed gaze. 'It wasn't stupid. It was lovely.'

'Too soon?'

If she agreed, it'd give him hope, but she'd made a complete fool of herself over Randy and wasn't in a hurry to repeat the experience. She couldn't see herself committing to any man again, even Charlie.

'Are we back to the 'never' thing again?' he persisted.

'Probably.'

'Seacrest really did a number on you, didn't he?'

Fran was startled. 'How did — '

'It was obvious by the things he said — or didn't — when he came in the shop looking for you.' Charlie's eyes narrowed. 'You did the same.' He caressed her shoulders, heating her skin in a single heartbeat. 'I was briefly engaged before I returned to Tresidder. Melissa broke it off because she didn't want a sandwich-shop owner for a husband.'

'That's awful!' The blunt confession broke through the protective wall she'd struggled to shore up.

'There's more to it than that, but it wasn't love, that's for sure.' Charlie's wry comment pulled a smile out of her. 'I never felt for Melissa a glimmer of what you arouse in me.'

Fran's breath caught in her throat.

'Don't say any more. Not tonight.'

He covered her mouth with his, drawing them into a sweet intoxicating kiss. 'But I'm not giving up.' Charlie pulled away and held her at arm's length.

'Good.'

'Norma Jean's getting lonely by now. We'd better go and keep her company.'

'You're mad.'

A huge grin spread over his handsome face, setting off happy sparks all through Fran's body. 'I think we've already established that fact.' He swung his long legs off the bench to stand up, and held out his hand. 'Come on, Cinderella. Your carriage awaits.'

'Please tell me you don't turn into a mouse at midnight.'

Charlie swept her into his arms. 'One night I'll keep you out late enough to find out.' He kissed her forehead. 'But for now, you'll have to guess.'

*   *   *

It reminded him of being a teenager. Parked outside a girl's house and hoping to snatch a kiss before her father chased him away.

'Yes, you've been good enough.' Fran's breathy voice made him shiver. This time she slipped her hands up through his hair, pulling him towards her. 'Just one.'

'Are we being spied on?' He nodded towards the house.

'Undoubtedly.'

'Remind me again how old we are.'

Fran's lips curved in a teasing smile. 'Old enough for this.'

When he resurfaced from their kiss, Charlie's head still spun.

'I'd better go.'

Her obvious reluctance cheered him, and he took a chance. 'Can we do this again?'

'The date or the kissing?'

'Both. Please.'

'Because you asked so nicely, I'll say yes. You can give up on the cake bombardment now.'

'Okay. I'll come up with something else to lure you in,' Charlie teased. He wanted to suggest tomorrow, but she'd made it clear that cool and noncommittal was the way to go. 'How about next Saturday?' A sliver of what might've been surprised regret crossed her face, but he didn't comment.

'Perfect.'

Like you. 'Norma Jean needs her beauty sleep.'

A curious little smile tugged at Fran's generous mouth. 'Fair enough.'

Charlie released her hands and got out of the car. 'I'll walk you in.'

'Lucy will be impressed.'

He chuckled, not about to tell her he'd already thought of that. They took their time wandering up the path and lingered at the front door.

'Good night, Prince Charming.'

Charlie bent down and cradled her foot with his hand. 'One day the glass slipper will fit, Cinderella.' He left Fran with her mouth gaping open.

Back in the car, he patted the steering wheel. 'What do you think, Norma Jean?' Charlie liked her positive answer and whistled as he drove away. He wasn't ready to go home for a few minutes, and decided to take the long way down around the quay and drive past Boscawen's Bites.

For a second, he thought he must be imagining things. He pulled into an empty parking spot and kept his eyes fixed on the shop window. There it was again — a glimmer of light that shouldn't be there. He hopped out and closed the car door quietly, then crept across the road to stand by the wall.

A shadow moved across his line of sight. The sensible thing would be to call the police, but by the time they arrived his thief would be long gone. He slipped down the alley between his shop and the ice-cream parlour next door. The back door was unlocked, and he cautiously stepped inside.

'What the — '

'Mr. B, what're you doing here?' Robbie froze in the middle of the room.

'I believe that's my line.' Charlie noticed the sandwich in the boy's hand

and a pile of pillows and blankets in the corner of the floor. 'You're sleeping here?'

'I can explain,' he stammered.

'I think you'd better.'

The colour leached from Robbie's grey face, and as he swayed on his feet, Charlie barely managed to catch him before he would've collapsed on the tiled floor.

13

While they waited for the coffee to brew, Charlie scrutinised Robbie. He'd noticed dark shadows under the boy's eyes the past week but put it down to being a typical teenage boy. Now he could tell there was more to his deep exhaustion than playing video games until midnight and getting up to start work at five in the morning.

He poured out a couple of large mugs and doctored Robbie's with plenty of cream and sugar. 'Get that down you and eat the sandwich. Then we'll talk.' Goodness knew how long it'd been since he'd eaten a proper meal.

'I wasn't stealing. I was gonna pay — '

'Do what you're told,' Charlie ordered. The boy slumped back in the chair, and he perched on one of the stools by the counter and sipped his coffee. 'Better?'

'Yeah.' Robbie stared down at the floor. 'Sorry.'

'Tell me everything.'

'I didn't have no choice,' he protested.

'Your mum threw you out?' Charlie took a stab in the dark.

'Not exactly.'

He reined in his frustration. 'Come on, Robbie, the whole truth.' The boy glanced up, and the utter misery in his deep brown eyes tore at Charlie.

'She's got a new boyfriend and he don't want me around.' A shadow of defiance darkened his thin features. 'I don't blame him. He's gonna marry her, and four kids is a lot to take on. I'm old enough to take care of myself.' He recited the explanation as though it'd been drummed into his head.

'How long have you been sleeping here?'

'Only a few nights.' The brief flash of truculence faded. 'I left home a couple

128

of weeks ago and I've mostly been kipping in the park.'

Right across from Charlie's house. His guilt intensified. 'Were you in here last weekend too?'

'Yeah. How'd you know?'

'I thought I was getting old and forgetful.' Charlie told him about the out-of-place chair and missing lemonade. For the first time, Robbie cracked a smile.

'Sorry about that. Course, you are a bit past it.'

'Watch it.'

'You going to call the police?'

Charlie stared in horror. 'Surely you can't think I'd do that?'

'I dunno. Wouldn't blame you,' Robbie mumbled. 'Breaking and entering. Theft. I'm guilty of both.'

'Did I or didn't I give you a key to this place?'

'Yeah, but — '

'But nothing. Haven't I always told you to help yourself to whatever you want in the way of food and drink?'

This time a tiny smile broke through Robbie's grimness. 'End of story.'

'Thanks. I'm all right now, so I'll clear out of here.' Robbie made a move to stand but Charlie pushed him back down.

'You aren't going anywhere until we've sorted out a few things. First we need to let your mum know where you are. She'll be worried.' Robbie snorted but didn't comment. 'If she's okay with it, you can stay at my place — we've got a spare bedroom.'

'But your parents — '

'They won't mind.' His mum would be happy to help but not his father. Charlie might have to do some grovelling to pull this off. 'Get your things. My car's outside.'

'The cool one?' Robbie's eyes gleamed. 'Did it impress your girl tonight?'

'Yes to your first question and maybe to the second.'

'You seeing her again?'

'What's this, twenty questions? I

don't need a teenager who's barely old enough to shave sorting out my love life.'

'I hope by the time I'm as ancient as you I'll have my act together better.' He poked Charlie's arm. 'We going to stay here arguing or go for a ride in your fancy wheels?'

'For all your cheek, I might make you walk,' Charlie retorted. 'Go out the back door and head out around while I lock up.' He couldn't help smiling. 'We don't want any sandwich thieves sneaking in.'

'Not that there's anything worth eating here.' Robbie's natural ebullience had returned.

On the drive home, Charlie wondered if this was his day for being rash. First he'd been idiotic enough to tell Fran he might love her, and now he'd offered his assistant a temporary home. He might end up regretting both.

★　★　★

A long, unappealing Sunday stretched out in front of Fran. She had assured Lucy and Patrick she'd find plenty to do when she turned down their offer of a day out in Penzance. She hated the fact they felt bound to invite her to join them when they went anywhere. They needed time alone, and she'd made sure they got it today even if she ended up bored to death.

She'd done her washing first thing and hung it out on the line to dry before tidying her room. Later on she'd ring her dad, but that still left a lot of unoccupied hours. Fran thumbed through the local bus timetable but couldn't work up the enthusiasm to go anywhere despite the lovely weather.

You could try to write. The idea of staring at a blank page or computer screen made her stomach hurt.

I suppose you've got to find a new way of working.

Yeah, I know, but it's hard.

I'm a good listener.

She struggled to talk herself out of ringing Charlie. He'd told her that his usual Sunday routine consisted of cooking a roast lunch for his parents before cleaning the shop and catching up on his accounts.

You could offer to help.

Fran startled as her phone buzzed with an incoming text message.

I know it's not Saturday yet, but summer days call for ice cream. Fancy coming down to get some with me?

For all of two seconds she debated the wisdom of accepting before texting him right back. *I'd love to. It's my weakness.*

I'll remember that. Meet me on the quay. 10 minutes?

Fran glanced down at the old red shorts and white T-shirt she'd thrown on this morning and decided they'd do. She ran upstairs and brushed her hair before adding a quick slick of red lipstick.

Outside, a light breeze whipped her

hair around her face, completely negating her tidying efforts in a matter of moments. She turned the corner onto the quayside and spotted Charlie. Before she could call out to him, a stunning redhead ran across the street and threw her arms around his neck before planting a kiss on his mouth. He made no effort to push the woman away, and they were soon engrossed in conversation. Fran angrily wiped away the tears burning her eyes.

She struggled to rationalise Charlie's behaviour with the way he'd been with her last night, but nothing fitted. After all, she hadn't backed Charlie into a corner and forced him to say he loved her.

Charlie laughed and gave the woman's corkscrew curls a playful tug. She pushed his arm away and ran off smiling. He glanced around, frowned, and stared at his phone.

Where are you?

Fran read the brief message and wondered what to do. It would be childish to turn around and go back home. She was a grown woman and could be mature about this. Plastering a smile on her face, she walked towards him.

'Hey, gorgeous.' Charlie reached out and wrapped his arms around her waist before she could stop him. 'For a minute there I thought you'd stood me up.'

'You weren't exactly bereft of company.' She kept her voice light and non-judgmental. 'Another fan of the Cake Romeo, I suppose? It's the Swiss roll that does it.'

'What are you . . . oh, you mean Anna?' A slight flush heated his skin. 'Anna's a good friend.'

I'll bet.

'She owns Kernow Choklat and made the delicious chocolates I brought the other day. She simply came over to thank me for sending some business her way. I talked up her shop to some of my suppliers, and several of them have placed big orders.'

'That's nice.' Fran worked hard at being generous but couldn't scrub the picture of the two of them from her head.

'I don't make a habit of telling one woman I love her and turn right around and kiss someone else.' Charlie's eyes darkened to a deep shade of indigo, the same as last night's sea after the sun went down. 'Do you believe me?'

If they were to develop any sort of long-term relationship, it couldn't be based on lies or half-truths. Did she trust him?

14

Charlie knew exactly what she'd seen and what it must've looked like, but that didn't ease his disappointment.

'Anna and I went to school together. The Tremayne family owns the Green Man, and her dad gave me my first kitchen job when I left school. Anna's one of my few real friends here outside of Patrick and Lucy, but there's never been anything romantic between us.'

'I'm sorry. I shouldn't have jumped to the wrong conclusion.'

He tilted her chin so she couldn't avoid his searching stare. 'I hope you're not just saying what you think I want to hear. Anna only kissed me because she was excited today, that's all.'

'I should've had faith in you.'

'Maybe I haven't earned it yet. We've both been around the block a few times, and life leaves scars. We're not teenagers.'

'Are you implying we're old?'

'I wouldn't dare,' Charlie joked. 'But you've got to admit I'm hardly your first boyfriend, and you're certainly not — '

'Stop right there.' Fran pressed her hand over his mouth. 'I really don't want to hear about your other conquests. You promised me ice cream, and it's time to deliver.'

He couldn't resist a lingering kiss, and by her enthusiastic response, she obviously didn't object. 'Now you get ice cream. Okay?' The soft-spoken question earned him a nod and one of her glorious smiles.

A few minutes later they were lucky enough to find an empty bench and sat licking their ice creams. He kept to himself that he'd easily guessed which flavour she'd choose, remembering her ambivalent reaction to his accurate lunch selections.

Lemon meringue ice cream sounded

more healthy and virtuous than his triple chocolate treat, but by the time she added a soft dollop of clotted cream and a crumbly chocolate Flake, there was little to choose between them.

'Any good?'

She rolled her eyes and sunk her teeth into another large bite.

'I'll take that as a yes,' Charlie teased. 'You're doing an excellent job of protecting it from the pesky gulls. Eating fast is the perfect solution.' He'd warned her about the vicious seagulls that specialised in dive-bombing unsuspecting visitors' ice creams.

'Are you implying I eat in an unladylike way?'

'Not at all. It's absolutely essential not to dawdle.'

Fran's wary glance said she was pretty sure he was making fun of her but would let him get away with it, at least for now. She finished the last bite and wiped her hands together. 'That was amazing. My hips might not survive a whole summer in Cornwall without exploding.'

To him, everything about Fran was perfect, but he kept that thought to himself.

'Why are you staring at me?'

Charlie didn't reply straight away.

'Remember, we're supposed to be doing the truth thing. Doesn't matter if it's about ice cream or — '

'Love.' Her skin reddened and Charlie wished he'd lied, or at least not been totally honest. 'I promised not to say that dangerous word again. Sorry. I only wanted to say eat as many ice creams as you like, because to me you'll still be beautiful.'

'How do you do it every time?'

'What?'

'Wrong-foot me. Throw me out of whack.' Fran grabbed hold of his hand. 'You're so . . . you.'

'I don't know how to be anything else.' Charlie admitted. 'I tried many times and failed miserably. If I hadn't been forced to come back here when Alex died, I'd have burned out in

London. I was on track to implode in a pretty spectacular way.'

'You were working too hard?'

He gave a caustic laugh. 'And the rest. My private life was a disaster.'

'What about Melissa?'

'I wasn't completely honest with you.' Charlie grimaced. 'It wasn't totally her fault we broke up, because I pretty much drove her to it.'

'But — '

'I neglected her. She should've been my priority, but getting another Michelin star topped my list. Nothing else mattered. I mistreated the people I worked with, and most only stayed for the prestige attached to the restaurant. I'm sure they hated me.' Everything poured out until his throat tightened and he rested his aching head in his hands.

'Shall we walk?' Fran wanted to get him away somewhere quiet because they'd attracted several curious stares. 'Come on.'

'Okay. If you want.' He hauled

himself up and gave her hand a squeeze. They wandered out towards the outer quay. 'Sorry for being a misery. It's not what you signed up for when I invited you for ice cream.'

'My Sunday was mind-numbingly dull until you rang. At least I'm not bored to death now.'

'Glad to hear I'm good for something.' Charlie's smile lit him from the inside out, reminding Fran of Edna Kittow's words.

All the women swoon over his searing blue eyes.

Naturally she'd checked up on Paul Hollywood and discovered that Edna knew what she was talking about. But after watching several episodes of the baking show, Fran was convinced Charlie easily beat the celebrity baker in both the good looks and cake departments.

'Now *you're* doing the staring thing. Do I have Flake crumbs stuck in my teeth?'

No, but you do have the most

gorgeous eyes, and your smile makes me melt. She managed to shake her head.

'Do I need to tickle you to get an honest answer?' He tightened his arms around her waist and soon had Fran squealing and begging for mercy.

'Let go! You smiled and I . . . find it attractive, that's all.' Fran's blush turned into an all-out scorch.

Charlie pressed a gentle kiss on her mouth. 'If it's any consolation, the feeling's mutual. I turn into a pathetic teenage boy around you.'

'Don't talk rot. You're not like any teenage boy I ever came across,' Fran protested. 'They were all really lame and immature.' She grimaced. 'Plus they never fancied me. I was too tall. Too mouthy. Too smart. Plus I wasn't willing to boost their egos by pretending to be dumb.' She'd never understood why her equally clever friends turned into simpering, spineless creatures when a spotty boy paid attention to them.

The crinkles around his eyes deepened. 'I'm not laughing *at* you, love. I'm feeling sorry for the poor boys who didn't know what to make of you. You were way out of their league. I'm happy to admit I fancy you like crazy and old enough to appreciate a smart, confident woman.'

'Is that how you see me?' She registered his bemused surprise at her unexpected question.

'Of course.'

'There's no 'of course' about it.'

'There is from where I'm standing.'

'Oh,' Fran croaked.

'I know you had a tough time, but you picked yourself up and kept going.'

'But I'm not writing,' she protested.

'You will.' Charlie's confidence stunned her. 'Have you had any ideas since you've been here?'

'Apart from drooling over you?' Fran joked.

He stopped walking and turned to face her so she couldn't avoid his intense gaze. 'Don't use my lame defence mechanism. I'm the master of deflecting anything serious with a smile and a wink.'

'Why do you do it?' She'd turned the tables on him, partly to find out the truth but also to avoid talking about her own elephant in the room.

'I'll happily answer you, but then we're going back to what we were really talking about.' Charlie's gentle admonition struck a nerve. 'When I came back to Tresidder, I wasn't in a good place to be in a relationship with anyone.' His attempt at a smile disappeared. 'I came to the conclusion the safest way was to be friendly with everybody without letting people get too close. I told myself that once the business was back on its feet, I'd reconsider.'

'Lonely.'

'Maybe. But safe.' His indifferent shrug didn't match the dark shadows sucking away the brightness from his eyes. He glanced at his watch. 'I didn't realise how late it was. I need to get back to the café and give Robbie a hand with the cleaning. He's doing penance today, and I expect he's worn his fingers to the bone by now.'

'Why?' Fran listened as he told her the whole story of the boy's sort-of break-in. 'That's awful. You did the right thing.'

'My dad doesn't think so, but I expected him to oppose the idea.' He kicked a stone, not quite looking at her. 'He says I've no right to bring juvenile delinquents into his house.' He glanced back up, his eyes brimming over with frustration. 'It took every ounce of self-control not to remind him that without me making the business profitable again, they wouldn't still have a home.'

'You're a good man. Why don't I come along and you can introduce me to your pet reprobate?'

'He's not — '

'I'm teasing, you silly man.'

Charlie looked shamefaced. 'Sorry. Out of practice.'

They walked back towards the

harbour and Fran's phone buzzed. She pulled it from her pocket and read the new text message.

Cute pink shirt. New boyfriend? RS.

She glanced around but couldn't see any sign of Randy.

'What's wrong, love?'

See you tomorrow. Expecting synopsis and first three chapters. At least.

'Fran, what's going on? You're worrying me.'

From far away, she registered the concern laced through Charlie's voice.

'You're not going to faint, are you?'

'Of course not.' Fran's protest did nothing to mitigate the frown that'd settled between his eyes.

'Seacrest?'

'How did you guess?'

'He's the only person who worries you this much.' Charlie shrugged. 'Are you going to tell me what he said?'

Good question. Was she?

15

'Randy's asking about the progress on my book.'

A leaden disappointment settled in Charlie's stomach. He'd watched Fran's smile turn to panic as she'd jerked her head around.

'If you don't mind, I'll meet Robbie properly another day. I know you've got work you should be doing, and I ought to go. I'm thinking of cooking a meal for Lucy and Patrick tonight as a surprise. They've been so good to me.'

The faint tremor in her voice convinced Charlie he was being lied to. *I'd have pushed all my work aside to spend more time with you.* Fran coloured up and glanced away. Their mental telepathy worked both ways, and she'd heard the words he hadn't dared say out loud.

'Fair enough.'

They walked back in silence, and as they reached the corner Charlie sensed her hesitation.

Go on. Tell me everything Randy said. Prove we've got something worthwhile going on here.

'Thanks for the ice cream.' She popped a swift kiss on his cheek. 'I'll see you soon.' She ran off before he could challenge her.

That told you. He briefly clung to the hope that she might change her mind and ring him later to apologise. *And maybe those annoying earthbound pigs will sprout wings.* Charlie exhaled a weary sigh and slogged along the road towards the shop, crossing over to avoid a couple of people he wasn't in the mood to talk to. Robbie had stopped in the middle of cleaning the windows to lean against the open door and talk to Anna.

'How's my favourite baker?' she yelled, her face breaking into a wide smile. He could do with soaking up a dose of her positive attitude.

'Surviving. How's my favourite chocolatier?'

'Much better with all the new orders I've got.'

'Happy I could help.'

'Robbie told me you were out on a date. Anyone I know?' Her warm brown eyes gleamed with unabashed curiosity. 'I was close to worming it out of him when you turned up. Now I can get it from the horse's mouth instead.'

'Don't get excited. It wasn't anything serious, just ice cream and a walk on the quay. Don't plan on being my best man, or woman, anytime soon.' His careful dismissal didn't fly with Anna, and she gave him one of her rare disapproving stares. 'Don't try your ice queen act on me.' Her continued silence irked him, and he threw his arms in the air. 'Okay, I give up. Her name's Fran Miller. She — '

'Is Dr. Patrick's temporary reception-ist and Lucy's old school friend who lives in California and is a successful author,' Anna rattled off Fran's resume.

'I guessed it might be. Attractive, clever, single. Perfect.' She tapped Robbie's arm. 'What do you think of Wonder Woman?'

'That's enough,' Charlie snapped. 'I'm not discussing my personal life with just — '

'Anyone?' Robbie, red-faced and annoyed, finished his sentence. 'Stupid me, thinking you was different. Put me back in my place, why don't you? You can stick your stupid job and crummy bedroom, cause I don't need them.' He threw the sponge in the bucket, and soapy water splashed all over the pavement. Then he ripped off his work apron and tossed it at Charlie's feet.

'Don't be daft. I'm sorry. I didn't — '

'Oh save it. You can flaming well join the long list of people who don't want me around.' With that, he ran off down the street.

'What the — '

'Let him go.' Anna gripped Charlie's arm to stop him from chasing after the boy.

'What did he tell you before I came along and messed things up?' Anna had always been kind to Robbie, and he suspected she knew more than a little of his story.

'I can't really say.'

'Can't or won't?'

'You need to ask your father.' Her awkwardness increased, and Charlie's mind raced with trying to fit it all together.

'My father? What's he got to do with this?' The pieces slipped into place. 'Please tell me Dad didn't have a go at Robbie?' Her silence confirmed his worst fears. 'When?' He fought to hold on to his temper.

'After you left today to meet Fran.' The compassion in Anna's eyes ripped at him. 'We talked some about it and I convinced Robbie you'd stick up for him.'

'And instead I blasted him out.'

'Pretty much.' She shrugged. 'He's too young to understand you were mad at someone else and took it out on him instead.'

'No, he's not too young. People have been doing the same thing to him all his life. That's another reason why I should've held my tongue.' Charlie's fists tightened, pressing into his thighs.

'Don't go home right away or you'll say things you might regret later,' she pleaded. 'Let's go inside and I'll make us a cup of tea.'

'I've got work to do,' he muttered, 'and I'm not fit company.'

'I know all that.' Anna's soothing smile eased his anger. 'We'll have tea and then I'll give you a hand.' A hint of mischief played with the corners of her lips. 'You can tell me all about Wonder Woman.'

He dragged out something resembling a smile. 'Deal.' He reached for her hand. 'Let's put the kettle on.'

★ ★ ★

Fran hadn't been this agitated since the night she'd broken things off with Randy. Now another man was the root cause of the jangling nerves threatening to drive her crazy. The disappointment etched into Charlie's face wouldn't leave her alone. He was intuitive when it came to her and knew she hadn't come close to telling him the truth.

It wasn't hard to rationalise Randy's behaviour now she'd stopping panicking. Until she could get out of their contract, he was still her agent. His cut of her twelve-book publishing deal formed a big chunk of his paycheque every month, and she couldn't blame him for being concerned about her writing — or lack of it. That was his job.

But with any other author, he'd have taken the trouble to discover why they were having trouble getting their book turned in on time and helped them sort it out. Part of her inability to write could be chalked up to grief, but she and Randy both knew *he* was the main problem. The humiliation of being faced with pictures of him with Fran's fellow author Emily Van Doss plastered all over the Sunday newspapers had killed her muse stone dead. When she'd challenged him Randy claimed they'd attended the literary awards event purely on a professional basis, but their body language showed that to be an obvious lie.

Emily, ten years younger than Fran and absolutely stunning, was the newest star in the publishing world. The first-time author had shot to the top of the bestseller charts, and her psychological thriller was turned into a blockbuster Hollywood film. Emily had taken Fran's place as Randy's top client, and he'd switched allegiance faster than a vegetarian tempted by the mouth-watering smell of bacon frying.

A seed of slow-burning indignation curled up through Fran, and she reached for her laptop.

'Noxious November,' she typed. 'A literary agent slowly kills off his clients until there is only one left. Can Nora realise before it's too late that her agent isn't quite what he seems, and live long enough to bring him to justice?'

After three exhilarating hours, Fran's throbbing head forced her to stop typing. She attempted to straighten up, but her shoulders protested, and she patiently did gentle rolls and wiggles until the muscles unravelled.

You will. Charlie's confident reply when she'd expressed her doubts about being able to write again slammed back into her. He'd been on her side since the day they'd met, and she'd rewarded him by lying when it really mattered.

She ought to go and see him right now to apologise, but the story drew her back. It was always this way. Once the ideas started to flow, she dared not ignore them, because they resembled the elusive Cornish sunshine and didn't always hang around for long.

Fran heard someone moving around downstairs. 'We're back,' Lucy called up the stairs, 'and we've brought pizza.'

After getting engrossed in her writing, she'd forgotten all about the half-hearted claim she'd made to Charlie about cooking dinner.

'Extra peppers and salami. Your favourite.'

Fran smiled to herself. Her old friend knew her weaknesses.

'Coming.' She shoved on her abandoned flip-flops and tugged on a cardigan over her T-shirt before heading down.

'Patrick bought a nice bottle of wine for you both to enjoy.' Lucy's nose wrinkled in distaste. 'I get a gourmet lemonade.' She patted her stomach with a wry grin. 'This baby better be worth it.'

Fran didn't take the complaint seriously, and neither did Patrick, by his indulgent smile. She helped herself to a couple of steaming hot slices of pizza and sat cross-legged on the floor by the sofa. Lucy frowned as she crammed in a large mouthful. 'What? I'm hungry. Sorry if my manners aren't up to your standards.'

'I don't care how you eat. What I want to know is what you did to upset Charlie.'

'Charlie?' Her face reddened. 'What do you mean?'

Lucy set down her own plate. 'We saw him inside the shop when we were driving home and stopped to say hello. Anna Tremayne was there too.'

She would be.

'When I asked Charlie if he'd seen you, he turned all stiff and weird and didn't answer me.'

Patrick glared. 'Lucy, you promised not to — '

'Oh don't be such a fuddy-duddy.' She switched her attention back to Fran. 'And before you tell me to mind my own business, it *is* my business. I love you both, and anyone can see you're made for each other.'

'For goodness sake, you're living in a dream world. Not everyone's as lucky as you.' Her friend's eyes darkened, and Fran prepared herself to be on the sharp end of one of Lucy's rare tempers.

'Most people have to make their own luck.' Lucy grabbed Patrick's arm. 'Do you seriously think we'd have ever made it down the aisle if I'd left it up to this one? Talk about dragging his heels.' She squashed Patrick's attempt to protest with a loud smacking kiss.

'Married! Are you mad?'

Lucy shrugged. 'I might be rushing things a bit, but — '

'You think so?' Fran's sarcasm wasn't lost on her old friend. 'Look, it's been a long day. I'm going to have an early night.' She headed towards the kitchen with her dirty dishes. 'I'll see you in the morning.'

'I'll find out what went on,' Lucy yelled after her. 'I have my ways.'

That was exactly what Fran was afraid of.

16

Keeping a smile on his face today strained Charlie's acting abilities to the limit. Not only was it Monday, everyone's least favourite day of the week, but he had no assistant to help with the mountain of work.

Despite Anna's warning, he'd rowed with his father last night, and the memory left a sour taste in his mouth. At first, George Boscawen denied everything before getting defensive and calling Robbie a lazy scrounger. That pushed Charlie over the edge and he'd let his father have it. His only lingering regret was the distress their argument caused his mother.

At lunch time, he'd glanced up hopefully every time the shop bell tinkled, but Fran didn't put in an appearance, and by five o'clock he gave up. He started to tidy around, and half an hour later flipped the Closed sign over with relief. He couldn't help worrying about Robbie and wondering if the boy was safe.

Feeling sorry for him won't do any good. Do something positive.

Alex again. He cracked a smile at his brother's persistence. They'd hardly spoken in the months before his twin died, but now he'd taken up residence in Charlie's head.

'All right, you stubborn devil. I'll go and see his mother. Will that keep you quiet?' He hoped no one walking by outside could hear his shouted conversation with himself. Charlie finished restocking the chilled cabinets and locked up. He'd set his alarm an hour earlier tomorrow to get a head start on managing all the baking alone. It was a good thing he wasn't involved with Fran any longer, because he didn't have time for a social life. *Yeah, tell yourself that, you twit.*

A brisk five-minute walk landed him outside Robbie's door.

'Whatever you're selling, I don't . . . Oh, Mr. Boscawen. What can I do for you?' Vera Giles looked puzzled. She wasn't one of his regular customers, and they'd only ever spoken in passing around the village.

'I wonder if I could speak to Robbie?' He'd pretend ignorance and see what response he got.

'He's not here.' She stared down at the worn carpet under her feet, and her thin hands worked at the hem of her shapeless grey cardigan.

'Do you know where he is? He didn't turn up at work today.'

'What's up, love?' A big scowling man appeared in the dingy hall, and Vera's stumbled explanation further darkened the man's expression. 'The boy's gone, and good riddance.' He planted a beefy hand on Vera's shoulder. 'Done enough for him, she has, and it's time he fended for himself. The boy's seventeen, after all.'

Charlie reined in his anger. Mrs. Giles couldn't be blamed for wanting to share the burden of taking care of her family, but Robbie's last bitter words sliced through his attempt to show the woman any real compassion.

You can flaming well join the long list of people who don't want me around.

A parent's top priority was to care for their child, protect them and encourage them to find their place in the world when they were ready. That might be idealistic, and his own father was hardly a shining example, but even so . . .

'I'm concerned because Robbie and I had . . . words yesterday,' Charlie laid the blame on himself. 'He's been staying at my house for a few days but he didn't come back last night. I don't suppose you've got any idea where he might've gone?'

'Hopefully John O'Groats.' The man's harsh laugh irked Charlie.

'Are there any relatives who might have taken him in?'

Vera Giles shook her head. 'We haven't got no one. Do you think he's all right?' Her pale blue eyes swam with tears.

'I hope so.'

'Will you try to find him? Please.' Vera glanced at her boyfriend and back at Charlie. 'Come back and tell me what you find out.'

'I'll do my best,' Charlie promised, taken aback by her sudden flash of bravery. 'I'll be in touch.'

'We're about to have our tea,' the man grunted.

'Of course. I'm sorry to have bothered you.' He dragged out a vestige of good manners and left before the door could be slammed in his face.

All the way home, he ran though ideas in his head. Where did he start his search for a runaway teenager?

★ ★ ★

'Change of profession or research for a new book?' Randy's booming voice filled the empty waiting room.

Fran startled and jerked her head up.

He leaned against the doorway and flashed one of the smiles she used to find irresistible.

'Lost your tongue, or giving me the silent treatment?' He strolled across and hitched his leg up to perch on the edge of the desk.

'How did you find me?'

'Wasn't hard, darlin'.' He tapped the side of his nose. 'Just gotta ask the right questions.'

Fran supposed it didn't matter now. Face to face again after two months, the bitter resentment she'd been clinging to loosened its grip. 'How's Emily?' His skin reddened, but the obvious sign of embarrassment didn't give her the pleasure she might've expected.

'She's fine.' Randy reached out for her hand but she pulled it away. 'Look, I'm real sorry. I never meant to — '

'Make a fool of me?'

'That's not — '

'Yes, it is.' Her calm declaration had the effect of making him stand back up. He shoved his hands in his jeans pockets and a sullen expression settled on his face. 'You convinced me that you loved me, and at the time I thought I loved you back.'

'At the time?'

'I know better now. Love shouldn't be doled out according to the ratings on a bestseller list.'

His frown deepened. 'You've met someone else.'

'That's neither here nor there.' Fran didn't confirm or deny it because she wasn't about to discuss Charlie.

'It's my fault you can't write, isn't it?'

'That's a big part. I was grieving for my mother and doubting my abilities to finish the Calendar Corpses series. I needed shoring up not tearing apart,' she murmured.

'Yeah, I see that now,' Randy admitted. 'I'm here to help you get back on track.'

'Are you afraid you won't get your money?' Fran joked before letting her smile fade away. 'I do understand. This is your livelihood. We've got a contract

and I should've been more professional.'

'So should I.'

'Yep, you should.' Her swift agreement made him smile. 'Believe it or
not, after your annoying text message
yesterday, I got cross, and that triggered
an idea. I knocked out a synopsis and
the first two chapters of *Noxious in
November* last night,' she declared,
pleased with herself.

'Don't tell me — it's about a famous
author murdering her agent.'

'Not exactly.' Fran blushed. 'He's the
murderer and his clients are the
victims.'

'Trust you.' His loud guffaw rever-
berated around the room, and she
wished he'd tone it down. The last
thing she needed was Patrick coming
out to see what was going on. 'You
gonna have the book done in time?'

'I doubt it. Sorry. Can you get me an
extension?' she pleaded. 'I'm working
here and can't let my friends down by
giving this up to write full-time.' Fran

explained the situation and made some quick calculations in her head. 'I'm guessing it'll be close to September before I have a rough first draft pulled together. Maybe I'll have it wrapped up by Christmas, if we're lucky.'

Randy nodded. 'Shouldn't be a problem if we pull our fingers out. We'll get the cover and marketing sorted and still manage to pull off your usual April release date.'

'Will Emily object to you spending more time on me?'

His smile faded. 'We're not together anymore ... not outside of our professional relationship.' He gave a small shrug. 'She decided it wasn't wise.'

'Smart woman,' Fran murmured. 'It's nothing against you personally, not exactly. I only mean it's rarely a good idea to mix the two.'

'Yeah, I know.' He rested a lingering look on her. 'I broke my long-time rule with you and should've learnt my lesson.' An awkward silence fell, and

Fran wasn't sure how to end the conversation.

'Boy, what an afternoon.' Patrick's door flew open and he hurried into the room, carrying his medical bag. 'Oh, I'm sorry.' He spotted Randy. 'Surgery is finished now. You'll have to make an appointment for tomorrow.'

'Good to meet you, Doc. Randy Seacrest. Fran's agent.'

Patrick shook his hand and simultaneously tossed her a quizzical look.

'I'm updating him on my progress on the new book,' she explained.

'Is there any?' he asked and immediately coloured up, plainly wishing he'd kept his mouth shut.

'Believe it or not, there is since last night.'

Patrick frowned. 'Do you need me to get a replacement so you'll have more time to write?'

'No, not at all.' Fran hurried on. 'I intend to stay at least until September, when that baby arrives.' She laughed. 'Anyway, I'm enjoying myself far too much. There's enough material here for a brand-new series of books.' Randy raised an eyebrow. 'I'm considering trying my hand at cosy mysteries for a change of pace. I'm tired of blood and gore and thinking on the lines of a modern Miss Marple.' She didn't say out loud that the deliciously eccentric Cassandra Raven only popped into her head while they were all talking. Randy had dealt with enough oddball writers to understand, but Patrick would probably label her as delusional.

'You're not to consider starting on that until you've got the December book out of your system,' Randy threatened.

Fran pressed her hand over her heart. 'I promise.'

'Are you staying in Tresidder, Mr. Seacrest?' Patrick asked.

'No, I'm at the Brookdale hotel in Truro.'

'Why don't we all have dinner together tonight? I know Lucy would love to meet you.'

'To prove I'm not the Big Bad Wolf?' Randy broke into a hearty laugh.

Fran protested. 'I never said — '

'Hey, I'm not blaming you. We both know I didn't treat you right.' He turned back to Patrick. 'I'd be delighted. Why don't we go out somewhere? My treat.'

'That's kind of you. Lucy probably won't want to go far, and the Green Man down on the quay serves decent food, if that suits you? Come back with us to the house now and we'll go out to eat when we're all ready.'

'Works for me.'

'I'll close up and be ready in a couple of minutes.' Fran began to go through her end-of-day routine, still slightly bemused by the turn of events. Charlie crept back into her head. He'd tried to help her yesterday, and now that things were getting back on track, she wished she'd faced it all head-on then instead of running away. Tomorrow she'd attempt to put things right with him and pray that he'd give her — and them — a second chance.

17

'I'm going out for a walk and might stop in for a quick pint,' Charlie told his mother, ignoring his father's sour expression. He wanted the chance to check out a few possible hiding spots around the village in case Robbie hadn't ventured far. It was probably too much to hope that the boy hadn't hopped on the first bus or hitched a lift out of Tresidder.

Slamming the front door behind him, Charlie hurried across the road and into the small park. He wandered around and stopped to talk to several people — a couple out walking their dog and a young mother throwing a ball to her son — but no one had seen Robbie. He headed on down the hill and poked around a few of the back alleys, more to convince himself he was actively doing something rather than because he really expected to find Robbie.

Today's gloomy weather had sent most of the visitors home early, which wasn't good for business. The main tourist season was short enough without the middle of July turning cold and rainy. At least it'd dried up now after another wet day, but the breeze whipping in from the sea made Charlie wish he'd worn something more substantial than his regular summer uniform of shorts and a T-shirt.

He abandoned his walk and dived into the Green Man, where he could combine warming up with getting a drink and asking around for Robbie.

'Pint of Tribute, Jase.' Charlie caught the barman's eye and snagged a stool while he waited. A burst of laughter from the other side of the room made him glance over his shoulder. He stared at the group of four people gathered around a table, tucking into plates of food and having a lively conversation.

Fran eating a meal out with Patrick and Lucy made sense, but why was she sitting next to Randy Seacrest and seeming completely at ease with his company?

'Earth to Charlie,' Jase said, poking his arm. 'Pretty one, isn't she?' he chuckled. 'Think I might need to take myself up to the doctor's tomorrow. Get me some treatment for this racing heartbeat.' He tapped his chest with a wide grin. 'Do you think she's hooked up with that loud American?'

She'd better not be. 'No clue.' Fran was the last person he wanted to talk about. 'I don't suppose you've seen Robbie Giles today?'

'Thought he was working for you?'

Charlie gave him the condensed version of what'd happened. 'I'm concerned about him.'

'You want to be careful.' Jase leaned forward with his elbows on the bar and lowered his voice. 'Robbie might be better off out of here. Had you heard his mother's marrying

Brian Dalby soon?'

'Yep. I met him when I stopped by the house earlier looking for Robbie.' Charlie grimaced. 'He wasn't exactly friendly.'

'People are divided about him. Some say he's doing a good job taking care of the family. Others aren't so sure.' Jase straightened up. 'Better get back to work. I'll give you a nod if I hear anything.'

'Cheers.' Charlie drained his pint. Hopefully he could get out of the pub before Fran spotted him.

★　★　★

'Anyone up for another drink?' Patrick offered. Do you want to give me a hand, Fran?'

'I'll go,' Randy piped up.

'I want you to stay here and talk to me.' Lucy beamed and winked at her husband. What were they up to now?

'It's okay, I don't mind.' She jumped to her feet and headed towards the bar, almost bumping into someone coming the other way. 'Sorry,' she apologised and glanced up, the breath leaving her body.

'Lucy said you wanted to talk to him,' Patrick muttered behind her shoulder. 'Seemed like a good chance.'

'Charlie,' she squeaked. Why had she been stupid enough to blab to Lucy last night? Maybe the three large glasses of chardonnay her friend had tipped down her had had something to do with it. Fran should've known Lucy wouldn't be able to resist interfering.

'I'll get the drinks.' Patrick scarpered before she could stop him.

'Sorry about that. I didn't know you were here.' The last thing she wanted was for Charlie to think she'd arranged this.

'Another Lucy scheme?'

'Yeah. How did you guess?'

'It doesn't take a rocket scientist.' Charlie's dry quip cut through their awkwardness, and they laughed together.

'I intended to come and apologise to you today,' she confessed, unable to hold back any longer.

'But?'

'I didn't.'

'I noticed.'

'Do you have to make this any harder than it already is?' she snapped.

Charlie's stance softened and he took hold of her hands, wrapping them with his own. The teasing brush of his fingers made Fran tingle all over. 'Hard is going thirty hours without seeing you.'

Her jaw gaped open.

'How about telling Patrick you won't need that glass of wine after all? I'll walk you home ... later.' A mischievous smile settled around his mouth.

Fran nodded. 'I ought to say goodnight to Lucy and Randy.' Charlie slid his arms in around her waist and drew her close. Very close. His thudding heartbeat echoed through his thin grey T-shirt.

'Why not give Patrick a message to pass on?'

'Good idea,' she rasped. 'You'll need to let go of me.'

'Pity.' She relished the regretful tone in his voice. His hands dropped back to his sides, and she stepped away to the bar.

'Don't tell me — you've got better things to do with the rest of your evening than hang around with us,' Patrick teased. 'Have fun.'

'Tell Lucy I'll see her later and — '

'Tell Randy you'll be in touch?'

Fran smiled. 'Yes, if you don't mind.'

'Not at all. Off you go.'

She didn't wait to be told twice, and hurried back to join Charlie. They walked slowly, hand in hand, over to the war memorial in the centre of the village.

'How about having a coffee at my shop?'

'You can't open up for — '

'Why not? It's mine,' Charlie tossed back at her. 'There's no point having a café if I can't use it to my advantage sometimes.' His skin flushed. 'I didn't mean . . . '

Fran reached up and kissed his warm cheek, the rasp of late-day stubble he hadn't got rid of after work teasing her lips. 'I know that. It's a great idea.' She tugged on his hand. 'Come on, Cake Romeo. Lead me to your leftovers.' Charlie muttered something under his breath, but she didn't ask him to repeat it.

★   ★   ★

He stifled a grin at Fran, sighing and frowning at the empty plate while obviously considering whether it'd be bad manners to lick the last few crumbs. She caught him out and half-heartedly glared.

'It would've been no good in the morning,' she protested. 'You can't sell stale muffins.'

'Absolutely not. You've done me a favour.' It'd been amusing to offer her the array of cakes left after a sluggish day of sales and see Fran turn into a little girl, debating the merits of a flaky cream horn compared to a particularly delicious strawberry tart. Eventually she'd settled on a dark chocolate espresso muffin with a sticky caramel drizzle and candied pecans. Charlie could've chosen it for her himself and saved a lot of time, but what would've been the fun in that?

While the coffee brewed, she hadn't let him speak until she'd apologised.

I'm too stubborn. The old saying about cutting off your nose to spite your face might have been written for me. Dad reminded me of it again last night. I wanted to share Randy's message with you but held back because I was determined to deal with it myself.

Charlie understood only too well, because he was the master of plodding away without asking for help or advice from anyone. Fran explained everything that'd gone on between her and Randy before she'd fled California and today.

You promised I'd be able to write again and you were right. The fact that I had to get extremely angry before the plot of a new book emerged is a bit disturbing, but whatever works!

'Now we're good again . . . We are good again aren't we?' Fran's worry showed in her deep frown.

'I'd say we're very good.' He leaned over to wipe a smudge of caramel from her cheek.

'Perfect. In that case it's *your* turn to tell *me* what's bugging you.'

'How do you know there's anything? Have you got a crystal ball tucked away somewhere?'

'Don't prevaricate.'

He took a swig of coffee, realising too late it'd turned cold and bitter while they spoke. 'After we, uh, parted ways yesterday I took my frustration out on Robbie, and now he's disappeared.' Charlie poured out the whole miserable tale and waited to be told off. Instead, Fran simply wrapped her hands around his, and the unconditional comfort meant more than any words. 'Any ideas what I can do?' he pleaded.

'Did Robbie ever mention any friends outside of Tresidder?'

'No. I got the impression he didn't have many.' He struggled to explain the boy's situation. 'The kid tried his best to help his family, but he often got into trouble and didn't get on well at school.' Remembering Robbie's unbridled happiness the first time he made a batch of scones on his own pained Charlie. 'He's finding his place in the kitchen the same way I did and I've been encouraging him to think about going to culinary school.'

'I'm guessing he looked up to you.'

'Fat lot of good that did with me turning on him.'

'Try not to beat yourself up. At least you tried to help, which is more than most people did.' Fran touched his cheek. 'Focus on what we can do to find him. What about any empty buildings around the village where he could hide out?'

Charlie shrugged. 'There are a few, but I wouldn't know where to start.'

A quiet smile crept over her face. 'You taught him a lot, and maybe he'll try to use that knowledge somewhere else.'

'What are you getting at?'

'Maybe Robbie will look for a job in another café or restaurant,' she explained slowly as if he wasn't quite the sharpest knife in the drawer. 'This is only a guess, because I don't know him, but I suspect he hasn't gone far. Why don't you ring around all the local food-related businesses and ask if anyone's been approached by Robbie or taken him on?'

'Surely they'd want references?'

Fran rolled her eyes. 'There's always a high turnover in your line of business and it's the peak of tourist season. Isn't everyone looking for staff to start work yesterday?'

He hated to admit she was right, but if he didn't get Robbie back soon, he'd be scrambling to take on someone else too. 'You're not simply a pretty face.'

'It's taken you this long to work that one out?'

No, I knew it the day we met. Something about you grabbed me by the throat and never let go.

Fran's gaze deepened. The saturated dark green of a ripe avocado, shiny and tempting. 'Dangerous, Charlie,' she drawled.

Tell me something I don't know.

'I'd better go now, but I'll come back tomorrow lunchtime so you can feed me and then get me up to date.'

'Don't I get a kiss first?' He stood up and offered her his hand.

'Out-of-this-world muffins and a kiss. I must've been a good girl.'

For his answer, Charlie drew her to him and made the world go away for a while.

18

The pre-dawn quiet suited Fran. Four o'clock and not even the birds were singing yet. She'd always done her best work before most people got out of bed. With luck, she'd get another couple of chapters written before it was time to get ready for her day job.

She leaned back in the chair and rested her hands behind her head. Allowing herself time to think about Charlie wasn't in the strict schedule she'd worked out to get her new book finished, but she deserved a reward. She could still conjure up the intoxicating lure of his kiss, drawing him to her last night as if he were a dying man and she his lifebelt. She wasn't certain he realised the saving was mutual.

Randy's reappearance put a lot of her demons to rest. He wasn't the ogre she'd made him out to be for a while, but he'd never been her knight in shining armour either. Instead he was simply a flawed man who couldn't love her the way she deserved.

And Charlie can? She couldn't answer the nagging voice in her head yet, but she rather thought she might be able to before very long.

Drawing on the self-discipline she'd relied on for the last decade, she forced herself to stop daydreaming and get back to pouring out the story that'd woken her an hour ago.

'Fran, are you all right? We hadn't heard you moving around, and Patrick's nearly ready to leave for the surgery,' Lucy's voice poked through the sleepy fog.

Fran lifted her head from the table. 'Oh, come in.'

'Don't tell me you haven't been to bed?'

'Of course I have. I got up early, that's all.'

'How early?'

'Three a.m. Happy now?'

'You are certifiably mad!'

'It comes with the territory.' She shrugged. 'You hassled me about getting back to writing, and now I am. This is what it looks like.' Struggling to her feet, Fran yawned and stretched out her stiff arms. 'I'll be fine.' She glanced at the clock. 'Oh no! Tell Patrick to go on without me and promise him I'll be there by eight.'

'You won't make it unless you fly.' Lucy chuckled.

'Trust me.' She grabbed her friend by the shoulders and steered her towards the door. 'Shoo. Go and eat your breakfast. Don't worry about fixing anything for me.'

'You really love writing, don't you?' Lucy's sharp blue eyes fixed on Fran.

'Yeah. I do. I simply forgot that for a while. If I hadn't come here . . . ' She stumbled for the right words to express her gratitude.

They hugged, and for a few moments the years fell away as they returned to their old wonderful closeness.

187

'But you did come, and that's all that matters,' Lucy whispered. 'Oh!' She grinned at Fran. 'Did you feel that?'

'What the — '

'Ewan's kicking like crazy this morning.'

'Ewan? It's a boy?'

'No, we're going to call our daughter Ewan,' she retorted. 'Of course it's a boy. Ewan Patrick Hunt. Why do you think Patrick's been going around with a silly smile on his face since our appointment last week?' She reddened. 'We changed our minds about not wanting to know, but we haven't told anyone else yet, so keep it to yourself please.'

Fran hated the flash of envy consuming her. 'That's wonderful.'

'It certainly is. I'm sure one day you'll — '

'Don't,' she pleaded. 'You don't know what you're saying.'

'Then tell me.' Lucy's expression hardened. 'I want the truth this time, not some half-baked version.'

'I'll be late for work. We can — '

'If Patrick gets mad, you can blame me. Talk,' Lucy ordered.

Hesitantly at first, before changing into a torrent of words, the story she hadn't told anyone else besides her parents emerged. The broken-hearted sympathy glistening in her friend's eyes made Fran weep.

★　★　★

Charlie prepared a special lunch box, but by one o'clock there was still no sign of Fran. He was dying to tell her what he'd discovered about Robbie, but more than anything he ached to see her again. If she broke her promise, Charlie knew it would be for a good reason. Doctors had emergencies — it was the nature of the job — and she might've got caught up with helping Patrick. Between customers, he eagerly checked his phone. Nothing.

Earlier he'd made numerous fruitless phone calls to all the local cafés and restaurants before getting desperate and widening his search. Charlie rang an old classmate from culinary school who'd recently opened a bistro in St. Ives, Harry Sales; and as soon as he mentioned Robbie's name, Harry admitted he'd hired him the day before.

He's a good kid. You trained him well and I'm surprised you let him go. He's a hard worker.

Charlie told Harry the bare bones of the story and asked him not to mention their phone call. *All right if I stop by tonight to see him? It'll be around half past seven before I can get there.*

Of course. It'd be great to see you again. I'm fully booked, but I'll squeeze you in for dinner. Bring a friend if you like. I'll have a table for two ready.

There was no way he could force Robbie to come back, but Charlie wanted the chance to explain himself. If nothing else, he could reassure Mrs. Giles that her son was safe and in good hands. He'd thought of inviting Fran to come with him but wasn't sure what to do now.

'Sorry I'm late.' Fran rushed in, looking harassed and pushing a loose strand of hair away from her eyes.

The shop was empty, and Charlie would've sneaked around the counter to give her a kiss, but something about her strained manner held him back. 'Is everything all right? You look . . . tired.' That was the most tactful way he could phrase it, because she wouldn't appreciate him pointing out her colourless skin and dull, worried eyes.

'I got up early to write. Really early.'

'That's good. Is it going well?'

'I guess.'

The conversation faltered and he noticed Fran sneak a glance at her watch. 'Are you in a hurry?' He missed last night's smiling, seductive woman and wished he could find the right thing to say and get her back.

'Yes. I've a lot to do before afternoon surgery starts.' She glanced at the display cabinet. 'What've you got left?'

'This.' He reached behind him and

pulled out the reserved picnic box from the chilled cabinet. 'Personally designed to appeal to a very special lady.'

A brief hint of pleasure brightened her flat expression. 'Oh. I didn't expect — '

'You said you'd be in for lunch.'

'I know.' Fran fiddled with the ends of her hair.

He'd try a different tack and see where that got him. 'There's one bit of good news. I've tracked down Robbie.'

'That's cool. Where is he?'

Charlie rattled off the whole story. 'Would you like to come with me? It's a beautiful drive, and Harry's an awesome chef, so we'll be well fed.'

'I'm not sure.'

He wouldn't beg, but refused to give up on her — and them. 'What's up?' He left the box on the counter and walked out around. 'Did I do something wrong? If I did, then tell me and I'll try to put it right.' He grasped her hands, fighting the urge to kiss the nonsense out of her. 'Come on. We're better than this.'

'It's not you, it's — '

'Don't insult my intelligence,' he snapped, and Fran's eyes filled with tears. 'What is it, honey?'

'I honestly need to get back to work,' she pleaded. 'Look, I'll accept your dinner invitation and we can talk on the way.'

There were times to press, and others when taking a step back was the best decision. Charlie literally and figuratively stepped away before picking up the box again and holding it out in front of him. 'One exceptional lunch for a hungry lady.'

Fran's eyes shone. Fresh grilled asparagus drizzled with a buttery lemon sauce. One day he'd get her to roar with laughter when he confessed to his unusual description wheel. 'You're a star.' She pulled out her purse.

'Put your money away. This one's on me.' He breathed a sigh of relief when she didn't argue and gave him a proper smile.

'Thank you. In that case, it's my treat tonight,' she declared.

'I'm hoping our meal will be on the house after the number of times I bailed Harry out in culinary school. He wouldn't have got through our pastry classes without my help. The man's got leaden fingers when it comes to baking.'

'We'll see.' She took the box. 'It was sweet of you to fix this for me.'

'Sweet is my middle name,' Charlie joked. He must've been staring, because she self-consciously licked her top lip, rubbing off a layer of deep pink gloss. Strawberry icing on a Napoleon slice.

'Stop that.'

'Stop what?' He needed her to spell it out.

'The staring thing,' she mumbled.

'I will if that's what you really want.'

Fran shook her head.

'You have no idea how happy that makes me.' He dipped his head, brushing his mouth over hers to taste her soft lips and deepen the bloom on her skin. 'That might keep me going until tonight.' The shadow that'd surrounded her earlier made a brief reappearance, and Charlie spread his hands over her shoulders so she couldn't look away. 'Nothing can put me off you, okay?'

'You don't know that,' she whispered.

'Yes, I do. I'm sure you can't have done anything that's so bad I wouldn't understand.' He cracked a wry smile. 'I haven't exactly been a saint myself.'

'It's not something I've *done*. At least not exactly. It's a piece of information that could . . . change things between us. Or not.' The confusing statement bewildered him. 'Look, I've really got to go back to work.' Fran kissed his cheek. 'I'm sorry. I don't mean to be enigmatic.'

'Off you go, and eat your lunch. I'll pick you up at half-past six. I'm convinced we'll still be good.'

'I hope so, Charlie.'

He dredged up every last drop of self-control to let her go. He ached to run after her and plead for her to put him out of his misery now.

19

After changing clothes six times, Fran ended up back in the simple jade-green sundress she'd started out wearing an hour earlier. Thank goodness it'd been crazy busy at the surgery all afternoon, because she'd had no time to brood over Charlie. She'd lied about not being able to pick up her lunch any earlier. The truth was she'd almost chickened out, but in the end hadn't been able to break her promise. The second she walked into the shop, Charlie had stopped in the middle of making a sandwich and flashed a killer smile. It'd been downhill from there on. Which brought her to now.

Lucy insisted she was being an idiot and conjuring up problems where none existed. The trouble was, Fran always looked two steps ahead and planned things out. Tonight she intended to pre-empt one important question that Charlie was likely to ask one day.

'Your Cake Romeo is here!'

'I'll be right down.' Fran ran her trembling hands over her hips, ostensibly to smooth the dress but really in a hopeless effort to calm down. She took several hitching breaths and prepared to face him.

'He's a miserable so-and-so tonight,' Lucy complained.

'Only because I object to her calling me by that dumb name,' Charlie retorted. He spotted Fran and exhaled a long, low whistle. 'Wow!'

His heavy-lidded gaze trawled down over her, and she wondered why she'd bothered to apply blusher. A bucket of ice dumped on her head would be welcome right now.

'Cleans up well, doesn't she?'

'You could say that,' Charlie murmured, his searing blue eyes never leaving her.

'Shall we go?' Fran asked, and waved

her hand in front of his face. 'It's not polite to stare.'

'It's your fault for being so beautiful.' The matter-of-fact compliment stunned her into silence. 'Good night, Lucy.' He seized Fran's hand, and they were outside the door before she found her voice again.

'No wonder you've got a reputation.'

He stopped walking, and his stern expression made her tremble all over again. 'I meant every word I said in there. Don't compare it to the everyday light-hearted flirting I do with my customers. They're two totally different things.'

'I was joking,' Fran protested. It'd been a useless attempt to protect her heart, because he wasn't the only one wrong-footed tonight.

Charlie's soft blue shirt matched his eyes, and he'd rolled up the sleeves to expose his tanned forearms. His nubby linen trousers and tan leather sandals were smart but casual at the same time. His hair had soaked up the recent sun, but she noticed a few silvery threads woven through the thick blond streaks. She guessed he'd be one of those annoying men who only became more handsome as he aged.

'Can we please start again?' she begged. She had intended to hold him at arm's length until she'd said her piece, but his blatant admiration threw her for a loop.

'Of course. I shouldn't be so sensitive.'

She glanced past his shoulder. 'Oh goodie, you brought Norma Jean.'

The adorable crinkles around his eyes and mouth deepened. 'I'm lucky you're not jealous of her too.'

'I am not j — '

'Only joking,' he quipped. Fran couldn't resist pressing a swift kiss right on his mouth. 'Mmm, what did I do to deserve that?'

Simply be your own wonderful self. 'You arrived in a very pretty car to take me out on a beautiful summer evening.'

'My pleasure.' His reply, matching

her attempt to keep things light, didn't fool either of them. 'We'd better be going.' He opened the car door. 'It's a straight run once we get on the A30 and shouldn't take much more than an hour. Luckily the Seaside Bistro is on this side of St. Ives, so we should avoid the worst of the holiday traffic going into the town.'

'I haven't visited St. Ives in . . . must be twenty years,' Fran mused. 'Mum and Dad took me there once when we lived in Plymouth. I remember crying when a seagull pooped on my head.'

'A traumatic experience.' The wicked grin Charlie attached to his supposedly sympathetic comment earned him a well-deserved smack on the arm.

'Drive,' Fran ordered, buckling up her seat belt.

'Certainly, madam.' He doffed an imaginary chauffeur's hat and chuckled. 'Come on, Norma Jean, time to go to work.' The car slid smoothly away from the kerb, and for a while Fran simply enjoyed the ride. She sneaked frequent admiring glances at Charlie and smiled at his utterly contented expression, the same one she'd seen on her father's face many times and solely attributed to driving his precious car.

Charlie held his speed steady and waited. He wouldn't push, but wished Fran would hurry up with whatever she planned to tell him.

'Okay, I'll get on with it.'

'I didn't — '

'You didn't need to.' She sighed. 'It's on both our minds because I put it there.' She splayed her hands on her lap and he noticed them shake. 'Lucy says I shouldn't mention it yet. That it's too soon . . . '

Charlie gripped the wheel but didn't speak.

'It's not a big deal. Well, it is to me,' she tripped over her words. 'We've only been out a couple of times, and it's not as if we've declared our undying love.' She slapped a hand over her mouth. 'Oops, I didn't mean that I forgot *you* sort of did.'

'Fran, don't take this the wrong way, but I wasn't planning to propose marriage this week, or even next.' He managed a grin while a corner of his heart shrivelled up inside. Had she fretted herself into this state because she'd been afraid of exactly that? Talk about a confidence buster.

The colour seeped from her skin. 'Oh, Charlie, that's not what I'm getting at.' Her head drooped and the excruciating wait for her to carry on just about killed him.

He turned off the main road and headed towards St. Ives. 'We'll be at the restaurant in about ten minutes.'

'In other words, hurry up.'

'Oh, Fran,' he sighed.

'This is going to sound ridiculous, and there's no reason why you'd even be interested but — '

Charlie checked his rear-view mirror and jerked the car to a stop by the side of the road. 'Okay. I'm not making a habit of this, but do I have to kiss it out of you?' He forced on a smile to go with the pathetic attempt at a joke. Fran's eyes welled up with tears, finishing him off. He undid both their seat belts and eased her into his arms, holding her tight while she sobbed.

Keeping your mouth shut for once. Good idea, kid, Alex laughed in his ear.

'I can't have children.' She gulped for breath, snuggling deeper into his chest. 'There's no reason you should care — '

'Shush,' he implored. 'I do care. Very much.' He sat back and encouraged her to look at him. 'I care because you're hurting, not because it might or might not affect our future plans.' The words 'plans' and 'future' shook him slightly, but he ploughed on. 'Do you know for sure?'

'Yes.' Fran's barely audible answer struck him deep in the gut. 'I know men aren't big fans of hearing gory details about female problems.' Her cheeks burned. 'But let's say I had a lot of trouble as a teenager and in my twenties it got worse. In the end, the only way they could stop the debilitating pain was pretty radical surgery.' Her voice fractured.

'Did it cure the pain?'

'Yeah.'

Charlie pushed a lock of hair from her face, much lighter now the black dye was fading. 'Then that's all that matters.'

'That's easy to say, but — '

'No, it's not.' His firmness stopped her protest, and she stared at him. 'I don't mean to overstep the mark, but you started this conversation. I get where you're coming from, and I'm glad I mean enough to you . . . ' Now he was the one faltering.

'You do.' She brushed furiously at her eyes, rubbing mascara all over the place. 'I thought if I was up front, then you could back off before we got too involved.'

'You thought I could simply stop loving you with a click of my fingers?' He shook his head. 'Not going to happen, sweetheart.'

'But don't you want a family?'

'Define family. Do you know how many kids there are around the world looking for a good home? Or ones like Robbie needing a bit of guidance and an extra dose of love?' Charlie hesitated but didn't say any more. Another day he'd tell her about Alex's son.

'You aren't saying that simply to make me feel better?' A tentative smile lifted the worst of the dark shadows from Fran's face.

'I'm not that noble.'

'Oh yes you are, Charlie Boscawen, yes you are.' She drew them into a long, passionate kiss, putting to rest the gnawing worries she'd put him through today. 'I suppose we ought to hurry up.'

'Reluctantly, I have to go with a yes.' There was something else he needed to say, wise or not. 'That bit about not proposing this week or next . . . I want you to remember I didn't mention the week after that or next month or . . . you get the idea?'

Fran's smile blossomed. 'Oh yeah, I

get it all right. That's the best 'not a proposal' I've ever received.'

'Perfect. Let's leave it there for now. Um, don't take this the wrong way, but you might want to check your make-up.' She frowned. 'Ever heard of panda eyes?'

Fran pulled a mirror out of her handbag. 'Oh God, thank heavens you told me. I look frightful.' She wiped away the worst of the smudges and repaired the damage. 'Better?'

'Gorgeous.' He pressed a kiss on her nose. 'Let's go and surprise Robbie.' He kept his reservations about the upcoming meeting to himself, still not convinced he'd done the right thing in coming tonight. He cranked the car back up and set off.

'There it is.' Fran spotted the sign. 'Neat spot.'

In the middle of a row of small shops, the Seaside Bistro stood out. Its rough walls were painted a soft salmon pink, and all the necessities for a day at the beach from shrimp nets to a blue bucket and spade plus a garish purple flowery lilo were fixed all over the front wall.

'Good location. Harry's done all right for himself.' Charlie got out and took his time walking around to open Fran's door.

'It's going to be fine.'

He appreciated her effort to reassure him and reached for her hand, tucking it into the crook of his arm.

'What on earth are you doing here?' Robbie yelled as they walked in. He slammed the loaded tray he was carrying down on the nearest table and the packed room fell silent.

20

'What's going on?' Harry appeared from the kitchen. Bigger and brawnier than Charlie remembered, his old friend was sporting a bushy ginger beard these days, maybe to make up for his receding hairline. His round ruddy face lit up and he hurried over. 'Should have guessed you'd be out here causing trouble.'

'Sorry, mate. I think we startled Robbie.'

Harry's gaze shifted to check out the chaos at Robbie's table. Red wine dripped onto the floor from an overturned bottle. A blonde woman was dabbing at the spaghetti sauce splashed all down the front of her white dress while her companion picked peas off his lap before dropping them with obvious disgust onto the tablecloth.

Charlie stood back out of the way

while his friend restored a semblance of order, banishing Robbie to the kitchen before promising the couple a free meal and clearing up the mess.

'You'd better come back here with me before you put me out of business,' Harry joked. He led them into a small steamy kitchen where an attractive young woman stopped in the middle of plating desserts and stared at them with open curiosity. 'Demelza, love, I need you to waitress for a bit 'til Robbie gets himself back together.'

'No probs.' She'd plainly prefer to stay and listen, but took off her apron and disappeared into the restaurant, giving Charlie a lingering glance.

'You'd no right to tell *him* of all people I was here,' Robbie groused, launching into Harry.

'Didn't know it was a state secret, did I?'

Charlie held up his hands. 'Hey, cool it. Harry, if you don't mind, I'd like to talk to Robbie privately for a few minutes.'

'Help yourself.'

'Hey, either of you think of asking me first?' Robbie snapped. 'Maybe I don't want to talk to *you*.' He jerked a finger in Charlie's direction.

'Excuse me for interrupting.' All three of them stared at Fran, who'd been quietly standing behind him. 'Your mother's very worried about you, and we promised her we'd try to track you down to make sure you're all right.' She gestured at Charlie. 'I think you'll find this one wants to apologise. He knows he was an idiot.'

Robbie's wary expression softened into something resembling a smile. 'Yeah, well, he's that all right.'

'Take some drinks and go out on the back patio,' Harry suggested. 'There are a few chairs and you won't be in the way there.'

'Some water would be nice, Mr. Sales,' Fran suggested.

'Heck, love, no one calls me Mr. Sales. Not even my bank manager,' he chuckled. 'Harry will do fine, although these days some people go for Prince instead because of my striking resemblance to our dashing young royal.'

'I can quite see why, and I'm sure you have an equal amount of luck with the ladies.'

Harry's smile broadened. 'Shush. Don't go shouting it around. My girlfriend won't be happy.'

'Girlfriend? Who's the lucky lady?' Charlie asked.

'I am, and whatever he's been telling you, don't believe a word.' Demelza reappeared and fixed Charlie with a hard stare. 'I knew I was right.' She gave him a sharp poke. 'Why didn't you tell me my idol was coming here tonight? You're friends with 'Charming Charlie Boscawen' and didn't think to say anything?'

Charlie caught Fran's barely suppressed giggle.

'We're old mates from culinary school. He, um, well Robbie — '

'Robbie worked for me, and I came

to see how he's getting on here and check if this old reprobate's learned to cook at last.' Charlie pointed to the dessert table. 'Everything looks awesome. The sugar work is spot on. You must be the pastry chef, because no way those are Harry's work.'

'She's the best.' Harry beamed and put his arm around her.

'Don't be daft, Harry. I'm nowhere near as good as him. I've a long way to go yet.' Her earnestness touched Charlie and brought back fond memories of working with a renowned French pâtissier years ago to hone his own skills.

'I'll make sure to leave room to try a crème brûlée later,' he assured her. 'They're a favourite of mine and tricky to make.'

'You gonna talk to me or not?' Robbie groused, shoving his hands in his pockets and glaring. 'Some of us have got work to do.'

'Sorry.'

Harry held out three cold bottles of

sparkling water to Charlie. 'Ten minutes, mate, then you're coming back in to eat or I won't be able to hold your table.'

'Yes, sir.'

Robbie pushed the back door open with an exaggerated sigh. The kid wasn't going to make this easy.

★　★　★

Fran itched to bang their heads together. The two men sat on either side of her, with Robbie glaring sullenly at the ground while Charlie tapped his fingers on the wrought-iron table. This was going nowhere.

'Right.' They both stared at her. 'What did you come here for?' She pinned down Charlie.

'To apologise,' he muttered.

'Get on and do it then.' Her sharp response made Robbie snigger. 'And you aren't helping.' She rounded on the boy and his face reddened. 'You could be more appreciative of the fact Charlie cared enough to bother coming to find you.'

'I never meant to hurt your feelings,' Charlie explained. 'I had other things on my mind and took it out on you. My bad.'

'You going to admit it's more than ice cream and a walk on the quay now?' He grinned, and nodded in Fran's direction.

'Yeah, yeah.'

'I thought so.'

'My dad shouldn't have spoken to you that way.'

Robbie's eyes widened. 'He told you?'

'I winkled it out of him.' Charlie's expression turned grim. 'We had words.'

'How's me mum doing?'

Fran wondered how he'd answer the question, and couldn't help being impressed when Charlie carefully navigated around his visit to Vera Giles and the meeting with Brian Dalby. 'She's worried about you, Robbie.'

'Yeah, well, Dalby doesn't want me around any more than your dad does. Don't bother spinning me some made-up yarn either. I'm not stupid.'

'I never said you were.' Charlie cleared his throat. 'I'd planned to move out next year and buy my own house, but I really can't stay with my parents any longer now. I'll get a flat while I look around, and you can stay with me — if you want?'

Fran hadn't expected that and neither had the boy, judging by his stunned expression.

'Are you serious?'

'Of course. Have you given any more thought to culinary school?'

Fran squeezed Charlie's hand. 'One thing at a time,' she hinted, and caught Robbie's grateful smile.

'Sorry,' he said for at least the fourth time. 'Bit of advice, Robbie. Make sure to listen to smart women. You'll be glad you did. Tell me something — how on earth did you end up here, anyway? I called all kinds of places closer to

Tresidder and only rang Harry out of desperation.'

'Bought a train ticket to Penzance, didn't I? I saw a poster of St. Ives up in the station and changed me mind.' Robbie shrugged. 'Harry had put a card up in one of the shops looking for kitchen help and hadn't had no one else after the job. I'll be dropping Harry in it if I slope off back to your place.'

'Where would you prefer to work?' Fran asked. 'It's totally your choice.' She gave Charlie another nudge.

'Oh, definitely, of course it is.'

Robbie grinned. 'I'd rather be back with you. Harry's all right, but I dunno, I guess I'm used to your odd ways.'

'Odd?'

Fran ignored Charlie and carried on. 'Why don't we talk to Harry, and if it's all right with him, you could stay here until he finds a replacement? Perhaps give him a week to get something sorted.'

'Hey, you were right, she is clever.' Robbie's compliment touched her. Fran considered giving the boy a hug before deciding it'd embarrass him.

Charlie's eyes glittered. 'I know how to pick them.'

'I don't know about anyone else, but I'm starving. So far this isn't much of a dinner date,' Fran joked.

'I'd recommend starting with the crispy mackerel fillets, then maybe the Cornish-bred Aberdeen Angus ribeye steak for him, and the stone bass served with Cornish crab meat for you,' Robbie suggested.

Charlie's face expressed a mixture of pride and amusement. 'Sounds wonderful.'

Robbie coloured up. 'I could give you all the details, but I'm supposed to do that at the table. He's strict about things being done all proper-like. Harry's the same as you that way.'

'Quite right, too. Let's go and eat before Fran falls apart.'

'Harry wouldn't like that. Makes a mess of the place, and we've done enough of that tonight,' Robbie quipped. He pushed his chair back out of the way and stood up. 'I'm not good at this sort of sloppy stuff, but thanks,' he muttered.

'You're welcome.' Charlie's gruff raspy voice brought tears to Fran's eyes. The teenager scurried back into the restaurant, and for a few seconds they didn't move.

'All right?'

'I will be.' He touched her chin, tilting her towards him, and pressed a warm, lingering kiss on her mouth. 'You're one very special lady.'

'I happen to think you're pretty special too.'

'Glad we're in agreement.' The intensity of his dark smouldering eyes conflicted with his light-hearted tone.

'Your table's ready,' Harry shouted out from the kitchen. 'Get in here, Boscawen, and I'll show you what real food tastes like.'

'You learned how to cook at last?'

'Behave yourselves. You're like a pair of schoolboys.' Fran's chiding had no effect, and the two men continued their juvenile banter. She resorted to a silent quelling stare.

'Oops. We're in trouble,' Harry laughed. 'We'd better hurry up before Demelza joins in. We'll never stand a chance if they team up.'

Fran wagged her finger playfully. 'Feed me. Now.'

'You heard what she said. Lead us to our table,' Charlie begged.

As soon as they sat down and she had a glass of sparkling champagne in her hand, Fran relaxed for the first time that day. It hadn't been an easy couple of hours, but they'd got through it — together. She'd ring her father when they got back to Tresidder, because for the first time in weeks she actually wanted to tell him what was going on in her life and ask his advice. That'd always been her mum's job, but perhaps she needed to explore a new normal there too.

A delicious plate of crispy mackerel topped with pickled summer vegetables and a drizzle of basil oil appeared in front of her, and she pushed everything else aside.

21

Charlie ran ideas through his head as he made sandwiches on automatic pilot. Harry's new worker started on Thursday, which meant Robbie would be back in Tresidder at the weekend. Tracking down an available flat needed to be his top priority because he'd promised to find the youngster somewhere to live. This morning he'd gone to see Robbie's mother, and she'd been relieved to hear her oldest child was safe. Vera Giles was still confused about why Charlie wanted to take responsibility for Robbie, and he'd been very careful how he replied. He hadn't wanted to imply any negligence on her part or express his lingering reservations about Brian Dalby.

Define family. Do you know how many kids there are around the world looking for a good home? Or ones like

Robbie needing a bit of guidance and an extra dose of love?

When Fran had put him on the spot over whether he wanted a family of his own, Charlie had answered her without any hesitation. Last night he'd forced himself to think more deeply about her admission. Would he like to have children? Of course he would. But it wasn't a make-or-break thing in his mind, and faded into insignificance balanced against Fran's health.

Last night they'd made a sensible agreement not to see each other until the weekend. Tourist season was in full swing, which meant Charlie was knee-deep in work, plus Fran needed to spend every spare minute writing her next book. The problem was that so far it hadn't even been twelve hours, and Charlie was certain he wouldn't last until Friday.

His phone beeped with an incoming message. *Special picnic lunch box at noon? I'm so pathetic where you're concerned!*

Charlie's immediate reply went back with a smile attached. *I was trying to think of an excuse to come to the surgery without actually injuring myself. Will have perfect inspiring lunch ready.*

With inspiring kiss?

Do you even need to ask?

All of a sudden the shop filled up and interrupted their flirty conversation.

Sorry. I occasionally have annoying things called customers. The lunch rush has started. See you soon.

I hope we don't have to make do with an imaginary kiss.

Do you care if anyone sees us? I don't. Charlie's finger hesitated above the Send button before giving it a determined jab. He started to panic when Fran didn't reply. Surely he hadn't overstepped the line after last night?

Annoying thing called a patient came in. Answer is a definite no.

He scrolled back to reread his question and sagged with relief. *Roll on noon.*

Absolutely. xxx. Collecting them soon!

Robbie would laugh himself silly at the pair of them acting like besotted teenagers. Charlie couldn't even remember behaving that way in his distant youth. At that stage, he'd only been interested in girls in a casual friendly way, too intent on work and getting out of Cornwall to let any particular one hold him back.

Humming to himself, he quickly put together a box for Fran before another customer arrived. That forced him to get his act together and focus on making a crab baguette instead of mooning over a certain gorgeous jade-eyed lady.

* * *

Fran stepped out of the surgery, stifled a yawn and blinked in the bright sunshine. The lingering effects of going to bed at midnight and dragging herself up again at four to write were catching up on her. All she could hope was that a brisk stroll down the hill and a few sneaked kisses would give her a burst of energy to get through the rest of the day. She hurried along the street to Charlie's shop and held the door open for a customer who was leaving.

As she stepped inside, the sound of childish giggles made her stop. Fran froze and took in the scene in front of her. Charlie spotted her, but as he opened his mouth to speak, she turned on her heels and fled. Halfway up Pondhu Hill she finally slowed down, needing to catch her breath and calm down before reaching the surgery.

How could Charlie have lied to her?

'But don't you want a family?'

'Define family. Do you know how many kids there are around the world looking for a good home? Or ones like Robbie needing a bit of guidance and an extra dose of love?'

She desperately tried to rationalise what she'd seen, but couldn't dismiss the scene burned into her brain of

Charlie, with a broad grin all over his face, holding an adorable little boy in his arms. The toddler, with his shock of thick blond hair and bright blue eyes framed with dark lashes, was the absolute image of Charlie. The petite smartly dressed woman gazing adoringly up at the man Fran loved hadn't helped matters either.

Quickly working out the time difference, she swore under her breath. Her father loved her deeply, but being woken at four in the morning because of something non-life-threatening wouldn't go down well. She needed to wait at least a couple of hours to avoid getting bawled out.

She was thankful to discover Patrick's parking space still unoccupied, because she wasn't sure she could've faced him right now. When she checked her phone there were half a dozen missed calls and messages from Charlie but she turned it off and shoved the annoying object deep in the bottom of her bag. Fran's rumbling stomach reminded her that she'd missed out on lunch, and she dug around in Lucy's snack drawer for something to keep her going. With a life-saving bag of salted almonds open at the ready, she caught up with all the administrative work. There was still an hour to go before afternoon surgery, so she pulled out her personal laptop and turned it on. Killing off another character might work off some of her frustration.

★ ★ ★

Charlie slammed the door shut and flipped the sign to Closed. The combination of working without Robbie's help and a never-ending stream of customers had made for an endless afternoon. He could kick himself for not telling Fran about Alexandre last night, but the question of why she hadn't trusted him enough to wait and ask for an explanation gnawed at him.

It'd been a complete shock when Chantelle and Alexandre turned up at the shop without any warning. She'd demanded that her son be allowed to meet his grandparents, and Charlie managed to put her off for a few hours by settling them into a room at the Green Man. He'd promised to collect them at seven so they could all walk to the house together. He needed to somehow break the news to his parents first rather than simply turn up on their doorstep. His other priority was to tackle Fran and sort things out with her.

He glanced around the shop and decided to break the number-one rule of cooks the world over. It'd been drummed into him from his first job at the pub that cleaning the kitchen thoroughly and leaving everything ready for the next morning was non-negotiable. It didn't matter if you were tired, sick or hung over: ovens must be cleaned, surfaces scrubbed and supplies replenished.

A loud banging on the door startled Charlie and he saw Fran's pale face pressed up against the glass. She gestured for him to let her in but he didn't rush, needing a moment to collect his scrambled thoughts.

'This is a surprise.' As soon as he opened the door, the words tumbled out. 'Sorry, that was rude.'

'I deserve it.'

'No, you don't. I should've explained — '

'Please, let me speak,' she pleaded. 'I rang my dad a little while ago and he called me an idiot.'

'I think I like your father already, but he's not completely right. I'm an idiot too.' Charlie grabbed hold of her stiff hands and rubbed life back into them. 'Let's sit down and talk.' The ghost of a smile softened her worried expression. 'Water?' Charlie plucked two bottles from the display and handed her one. 'Do you mind letting me go first?'

'But — '

'Please?'

'I guess.'

'About four years ago my brother

Alex had a whirlwind romance during a holiday in France with Chantelle Bonet, the woman you saw me with at lunchtime.' Laying out his inadequacies wasn't easy. 'When he told me they'd eloped to get married, instead of congratulating him I asked if he'd thought seriously about whether she'd fit in here. Alex accused me of being selfish and claimed I was frightened he'd want to give up the business and move to France.'

'Was he right?'

'More right than wrong,' he admitted.

'I'm guessing the little boy is his son?'

'Yes.' Charlie couldn't help smiling. 'Alexandre's a neat kid. Today was the first time I'd seen him, and he's so like Alex — and me, I suppose, judging by your reaction.'

Her blush deepened. 'I don't get it. What about your parents? Haven't they seen him either?'

'They don't even know about him

yet,' Charlie confessed. 'I didn't until a few weeks ago, and I've been struggling with the news ever since. Chantelle hated living here after they married — trust me, I'm not proud to have been right about that. My father refused to let 'some interfering French woman ruin the family business with her fancy ideas', his words not mine. I'm sure he made life unbearable for her.'

'Poor girl.'

He rubbed at his eyes, tired of the whole mess. 'Chantelle's father got sick and she went home to help care for him. By that point she and Alex were struggling to keep their marriage intact.'

'Didn't the baby bring them back together?'

'It might've done.' Charlie blinked back tears. 'Alex decided to go and see her in an effort to patch things up, and he got across the Channel with no problems. It's about a two and a half hour drive from Roscoff to where Chantelle lives in St. Malo, but he didn't . . . ' His voice broke and Fran got up, coming over to wrap her arms around him. 'The weather was lousy and there was torrential rain that evening. A lorry lost control on the slick roads and hit Alex's car head on. He never stood a chance.'

'Oh, Charlie, I'm so sorry.' Fran's sympathy tore him apart, and he scooped her down to sit on his lap, burying his head in her shoulder.

'I still don't understand how you all didn't know about Alexandre.'

He pulled back slightly, hating the idea of diminishing himself in her eyes but refusing to be anything less than honest. 'My father had Alex's body brought back here and refused to let Chantelle attend the funeral.' He watched the horror sneak into Fran's unguarded expression. 'I should've stood up for her, but I didn't, and it shames me. She inherited what little money Alex had, and my father told her never to contact our family again. She reverted back to her maiden name and stayed living with her parents, keeping the fact she was pregnant a secret from us. I don't blame her, because she'd no reason to believe we'd welcome her child any more than she herself was welcomed.' He struggled to get past the emotion threatening to choke him. 'She'd apparently intended to surprise Alex with the news of her pregnancy when he arrived to see her, and hoped they could reconcile and make a go of things.'

'What made her get in touch now?'

'She felt guilty.' Charlie cracked a wry smile. 'Ironic, isn't it? We're the ones who should feel that way, not her. We exchanged a couple of letters, and I offered to visit her later in the year after the summer rush.'

'But she beat you to it?'

'Yep.'

Fran's eyes darkened. 'Do your parents know she's here?'

'No.' Charlie longed to ask her to come with him when he broke the news, but had to know something first.

'Why didn't you trust me?' His whispered question leached the colour from Fran's face.

22

The sad confusion in Charlie's voice hurt more than if he'd shouted. 'I honestly don't know. My dad asked me the same thing.'

'How did you answer him?'

Fran's embarrassment deepened. 'I said our . . . love was new.' She stumbled over the pathetic explanation. 'Of course he pestered me for every detail about you.'

'That must've made for an interesting conversation.' Charlie's dry response drew an unexpected laugh out of her. 'I'm surprised he hasn't hopped on a plane by now to come and check me out.'

Oh God, could this get any worse?

'He is?'

'Yeah, sort of,' she mumbled. 'He's got an interview with the Plymouth Aquarium on Friday, so he's not making a special trip.'

'Just combining it with meeting the man who's stolen his daughter's heart?' Charlie leaned back in the chair. 'I get that, but you still haven't really answered my question.'

'Wouldn't you have wondered if it was the other way around?' She went on the defensive and then backtracked. 'You know what I mean. If it'd been something similar . . . '

'I'm not sure. I hope I'd have hung around long enough to ask for an explanation.'

'Oh, Charlie, I can't rewind the clock. We don't get to make that choice, do we?' A slash of colour highlighted his cheekbones.

'Touché.'

'I didn't mean that unkindly, but certain things can't be undone no matter how much we wish they could.'

'I know, love.' Charlie leaned back in and kissed her. As the heat from his skin combined with a teasing drift of spicy aftershave and the ever present hint of lingering sweetness from his baking, a ripple of awareness surged through her.

'Can you forgive me?'

'Of course. You don't even have to ask. You've forgiven enough of my mistakes already. But I'll allow you to make amends by doing me a huge favour.' She must've looked wary, because his grin widened. 'It's nothing terrible. At least, I hope it won't be.'

'Go on. Tell me the worst.'

'Have you got the time to come home with me now? I really want you to meet my parents, and . . . it'd help to have your support when I tell them about Alexandre. I know you should be writing but I'm not sure I can do this alone.'

'Of course you don't even have to ask.' She parroted Charlie's response and they both managed to laugh.

'We'd better go, because I've got to make it back to the Green Man by seven.' He absentmindedly shoved his fingers up through his thick hair, making it stick up at the back, exactly the same as little Alexandre's had earlier. 'I need to grab some food from the fridge because I told Chantelle we'd all eat together.'

'Isn't that pushing it?'

'Maybe but feeding people is what I do.' He shrugged.

Fran didn't argue because a band of tension stretched across his smile, dimming it and travelling down his fingers to tap a repetitive rhythm on the table top. She jumped off his lap and stretched out her hand. 'I suspect it'll be easy to win your dad over — all I'll have to do is give him a few hints about my next book.'

His half-hearted attempt to smile didn't make it all the way up to his gorgeous blue eyes, but she played along.

★ ★ ★

Charlie caught his mother's eye and shared her obvious amusement. His usually taciturn father was positively fawning over Fran and was now making her sit in his favourite chair.

'There's something we need to talk about,' Charlie said.

George threw him a rare smile. 'If it's good news about you and this lovely lady, I couldn't be happier.'

'It's not,' he hurried to clarify himself. 'Not yet anyway. One day maybe — I hope . . . ' A rush of heat streaked up Fran's neck to turn her cheeks bright crimson. 'It's about Chantelle.'

'You had to spoil things, didn't you?'

Decades of practice allowed Charlie to let the sarcasm roll over him. Before he could lose his nerve, he quickly told his parents about Alexandre. Sweat beaded his mother's brow and her pale hands clutched at the arms of the chair.

'I don't believe a word,' his father blustered.

'Then believe this.' He pulled out the picture and thrust it in his face. Helen snatched it away and stared hungrily at her grandson.

'Oh my God, he's beautiful.' Tears trickled down her face. 'We haven't completely lost Alex after all.'

'I'm sorry, I'm so sorry.' His father shrivelled before Charlie's eyes, collapsing onto the sofa and muttering under his breath.

'It's going to be okay, Dad.' He patted his father's shoulder. 'If it's all right with you both, I've planned to pick up Chantelle and Alexandre at seven and bring them back here for a meal.'

'That'll be wonderful,' his mother answered immediately. 'We'd love to see them, wouldn't we, George?' She didn't wait for a reply. 'Go and fetch them, dear. If Fran doesn't mind, can you leave her here? She and your dad can talk about her books.'

'I'd be delighted,' Fran hurriedly agreed, and Charlie had never loved her more. 'Do you want me to warm up the quiches while you're gone?'

'That'd be great.' Charlie kissed her forehead. 'I won't be long.'

Outside the front door, he stood still for a moment and reeled in his nerves before setting off down the hill to bring his sister-in-law and nephew home where they belonged.

*   *   *

Every time Fran thought she'd come to terms with her inability to have children, something sent her careening back to square one. This time it arrived in the form of an adorable two-year-old with the same tousled blond hair and riveting sky-blue eyes as his handsome uncle. Somehow she held it together when Alexandre flung his pudgy arms around her and smacked a wet kiss on her cheek, but thankfully Charlie rescued her and swept the little boy up into his arms. Sympathy shadowed Helen's kind features, and Fran suspected that the other woman might've guessed her secret.

'*Tu as faim?*' Charlie asked the squirming toddler, and Fran's limited French stretched just enough to decide he was asking if Alexandre was hungry. Naturally the little boy nodded, and the two of them headed into the kitchen.

Chantelle touched Fran's arm. 'You are Charlie's woman?' She wasn't the only one waiting for Fran to answer, because his parents stopped talking to listen as well.

'Um, yes, I suppose so.'

The Frenchwoman's perfectly shaped eyebrows rose. 'You either are or you aren't. I hope you are, because he is a decent man. Alex always said so.'

'Did he really?' Fran couldn't waste the opportunity to find out more. 'I know it upsets Charlie that he and Alex weren't close friends when he died.'

'Ah, I thought so. I can see the sadness in his eyes.' Chantelle shook her head. 'They are exactly the same as my Alex's, and he could not hide from me either.' A tiny smile pulled at her mouth. 'But he did try sometimes.'

'Charlie does too, but I don't let him.'

They exchanged a conspiratorial smile, and Fran had the happy sensation of discovering a new friend. 'And yes, I am Charlie's woman.' The proud declaration earned her a kiss on the cheek from Chantelle. Fran glanced over her shoulder to see the man she loved standing in the kitchen doorway with a stupid grin plastered all over his face. 'Are we ready to eat?'

'Yes.' His voice wobbled. 'We'll have it in the kitchen, if no one minds. It'll be less messy, and I know Chantelle doesn't want to be too late getting this little monster to bed.'

'When do you have to leave Tresidder?' Helen asked.

'We can only stay until Friday this time, but I promise we'll be back again soon. Maybe you could visit us in St. Malo?'

'Oh, I don't know, George isn't very — '

'We'd love to.' His stern insistence

touched Fran. The boy's cherubic smile and innocent childish giggles had melted his grandfather's heart.

They all piled into the kitchen and crowded around the table, but Fran perched on a stool in the corner, brushing aside Charlie's offer to shift his chair for her to squeeze in. She would've preferred to leave without making a fuss, but kept quiet and nibbled a few bites of salad.

'Are you going to walk down with us?' Charlie came to stand by her and settled his warm hand on Fran's bare shoulder. A shiver of longing ran through her for what she couldn't have. Life wasn't simple or fair. She got that. But it still didn't stop her from wanting.

'I'll come with you part of the way, but if you don't mind I'll head on back to Lucy's then.' She faked a yawn. 'I didn't get much sleep last night and I've got a busy day on tap tomorrow.'

'You know I'd do anything to change things,' he whispered.

Fran nodded and blinked back tears.

'I love you, and we can make this work together.' When she didn't reply, a trace of disappointment shadowed his face. 'Don't make any plans for Friday evening, because we're going to sort this out.' He straightened up and gave her one of his dazzling smiles. 'Okay, let's get this little boy to bed.'

While Chantelle gathered up her son and made plans with Charlie to return the next day, Fran found herself briefly alone with his mother.

'I expect you'll say this is none of my business.' A twinkle lit up Helen's soft grey eyes. 'But Charlie's still my little boy, even if he is nearly forty. I can see you love each other, but — '

'I can't have children,' Fran blurted out.

'Oh, my dear, I'm sorry. I did wonder if it was something like that. Don't worry, I'm not going to trot out all the platitudes you've heard a thousand times before.'

'Thank you.' Over the years she'd heard every variation, and it didn't matter how logical they were; nothing helped. Fran managed, with only the occasional hitch in her voice, to tell Helen about her problems and the resulting surgery that'd put an end to her hopes for a baby of her own.

'I'm sorry. There's nothing I can say to make that any better, but what I do know is that I've never seen Charlie so happy. You're good for him. Please don't deprive yourselves of the chance of a wonderful life together because of one small drawback.'

Fran bit back the retort she would regret voicing later.

'I didn't mean it harshly, my dear. George isn't an easy man to live with,' she sighed. 'He's made mistakes and hasn't been the perfect husband or father by any stretch of the imagination, but — '

'You're trying to tell me loving someone is never easy and all relationships have their challenges. I know that. I'm not a child.'

'I've said enough.' Helen held up her

hands. 'Maybe too much. All I'm asking is for you to give Charlie a chance. You won't regret it.'

Won't I? And won't he? Fran wished she could be so certain.

23

'You all set for your date?' Robbie leaned on the sweeping brush and grinned across the shop at Charlie.

It'd been a shock when his father had cornered Charlie before he left to pick up Robbie from St. Ives and offered him the use of their spare bedroom again.

Only if the lad's okay about it. I know you haven't had time to fix up anything, and I heard you on the phone booking a room for him at the Green Man. There's no point wasting your money when there's empty space here.

That was as close to an apology as he'd get. They might never be the closest father and son on the planet, but relations between them were improving. If he found out for certain where he stood with Fran tonight, his life would be a million times better.

'You taking her somewhere fancy?'

Charlie laughed and swung a key in the air. 'The chocolate shop.'

'I get that. I'm only seventeen and haven't had a proper girlfriend, but I'm pretty sure that's a dumb idea.'

'Don't be so sure.' He wagged his finger. 'Fran raved about Anna's chocolate the other day, and said she couldn't imagine anything better than being locked in the shop overnight with free rein to eat anything she wanted.'

'You're going to lock her in?'

'Don't be an idiot.' Charlie shook his head. 'Anna's made a few special chocolates at my request, and I'm taking along a bottle of champagne.' This would either be his best idea in years or the absolute worst.

'Good luck. You're gonna need it.'

'Thanks for the vote of confidence,' he muttered. 'At least I don't get stuck spending the evening with my parents.'

'Hey, they're all right. Your dad's going to teach me how to play chess and your mum's making pasties. Better than fancy chocolate and champagne,' he good-naturedly mimicked Charlie.

The boy's enthusiasm tightened his throat. After an awkward first hour or so last night, Robbie had settled right in, and his father seemed to take him under his wing.

'You're probably right.'

'I know I am,' he replied. 'Hey, if you trust me to do it right, I can finish up here and lock up.'

'Thanks.' A niggle of doubt wormed into Charlie's head, but Robbie's stunned amazement convinced him it'd been the right response. 'There you go.' He handed over the keys. 'Check — '

'The fridges and freezers. Put out the rubbish. Close all the windows. Lock the front and back doors and set the alarm.'

'Glad it's sunk in.' He kept his appreciation light. 'I'll be off.'

Robbie nodded and went back to sweeping the floor. Their man-to-man moment was over.

* ★ ★

'When's Casanova arriving?' Lucy asked. One hand rested on her burgeoning stomach and the other dipped into a tub of buttered popcorn, her latest craving.

'He's not. I'm meeting him down on the quay. And don't ask me where we're going because I don't know.'

'Oh, excuse me. Obviously you're not expecting anything fancy.' Fran's casual denim skirt and navy T-shirt received a dismissive glance. 'Enjoy yourself. Patrick's at a boring garden show meeting and they usually end up having a drink in the Green Man. I'll probably be tucked up in bed by the time you get back.'

'Enjoy the peace.' She grabbed her bag and made for the front door.

'Tomorrow I want to hear every detail of your evening.' Fran slammed the door behind her without replying. *All I'm asking is for you to give Charlie a chance.*

She arrived at the quayside and hesitated at the sight of Charlie leaning against the railings. The nervous flutter in her stomach intensified as he waved and hurried towards her. She waited to be kissed, but he stood awkwardly in front of her with a slight wariness shading his sky-blue eyes. She reached up to link her hands behind his neck and slid her fingers under the collar of his open-necked white shirt to stroke warm skin. 'I've missed you.'

Charlie stared down at her. 'I wasn't sure . . . I thought — '

'That's a dangerous occupation where you're concerned,' she quipped. 'Why don't we go where you're taking me before we become tonight's entertainment?' The glorious summer evening had brought out a crowd of locals and visitors alike to wander around the picturesque harbour.

'Oh, right.' Charlie glanced around him. 'Let's give them something to really talk about first.' He flashed a wicked grin and wrapped Fran in his arms before proceeding to dip her backwards and swoop down for a long, lingering kiss. Then he swung her back up onto her feet with a satisfied expression. 'Now we'll go.'

'Wow, I don't know what you'll do for an encore to that little exhibition.'

'Wait and see,' he teased.

She'd never seen anyone look quite as smug, but didn't ask why.

They crossed the road and walked past Boscawen's Bites before stopping outside the chocolate shop. 'It's closed,' she said.

'Yep, I know.' He dug around in his trouser pocket to produce a set of keys.

'What on earth are you doing?'

He let go of her hand and unlocked the door. 'This is where we're going.'

'Anna — '

'Isn't here. You said you'd love to — '

'Be locked in here overnight, but — '

'I've already been called out once tonight by Robbie, so don't worry. No underhanded plans.' His smile wasn't standard-issue Charming Charlie, but rather the special private one he reserved for her. 'Simply as much chocolate as your heart desires, and maybe a few other treats if you're good.'

Fran followed him inside and noticed one of Anna's tables all decorated and standing out from the rest. 'Did you do that?'

'Not exactly.' He shifted from one foot to the other and the tops of his ears reddened. 'I made a few suggestions, but Anna put it together.' A delicate white lace cloth draped the circular table, and in the centre slim pink tapers were grouped in tiny blocks of sparkling crystal. Pale pink rosebuds nestled in a silver filigree dish, and their intoxicating scent perfumed the chocolate-laden air.

Fran crept closer and read her name and Charlie's spelled out in a variety of chocolates. 'Oh my goodness.'

'Champagne?'

'I expected — '

'To be pinned down for a serious conversation?'

'I guess so.' Fran's nervousness increased.

'I very much want to meet your father tomorrow.' Charlie's quiet determination rattled her. 'Are you going to ask me why?'

No, because I'm afraid of the answer.

'You aren't getting rid of me because of one small hurdle — '

'Small? How can you say it's . . . ' The brightness of his gaze, a mixture of overwhelming love, and a hint of frustration silenced her. Charlie tugged her closer and wrapped his arms around her waist. Her senses filled with his warmth and pushed the irrelevance away.

'Do you love me?'

'Of course I do.'

A contented smile crept over his face. 'Thought so, but I needed to be absolutely certain.'

'Before — '

'Before I do this.' He dropped to one knee and produced a small box in his right hand.

'But — '

'Shush, be quiet or I'll lose my nerve.'

The logical side of Fran wanted to stop him and ask if he really knew what he was doing, but the fairytale lover lurking inside of her yearned for the whole wonderful dream á la Cinderella and Prince Charming.

'Will you marry me? Let's make a life together, Fran, and I promise you won't regret it.'

A frisson of panic seeped through her, but Charlie's steady gaze never faltered, and gave her courage. 'Yes. Yes, please,' she whispered.

'I hope to God this fits. You can blame Lucy if it doesn't.' He seized her hand and slipped the ring into place.

'Lucy? You mean she — '

'Of course she knows,' he chuckled. 'Everyone needs a Fairy Godmother.'

'No wonder she turned up her nose at my choice of clothes.'

Charlie's searing blue eyes raked her from head to toe. 'As far as I'm concerned, you're perfect.' Fran finally got around to checking out the ring, and the stunning oval-cut emerald flanked by glittering diamonds winked back at her.

'It's absolutely gorgeous,' she sobbed.

'Lucy warned me you'd cry and said I mustn't let it bother me. She assured me it's a woman thing.'

'But what about — '

Charlie leapt to his feet and hugged her before she could get out the rest of the sentence. 'We've got Alexandre to love, and I'm pretty much stuck with looking out for Robbie too,' he chuckled.

'I don't ever want you to regret — '

'I could never regret you,' he promised. 'You're all I want.' He stroked her cheek. 'You. Anything else is bonus. I'm happy to adopt a whole horde of children if you want. We've got plenty of love to share.'

'We certainly do.' *Loving someone is never easy, and all relationships have their challenges.* Her own words returned to metaphorically smack her in the face. 'Now do I get to eat all this delicious chocolate?'

'All of it? You'll never find a wedding dress to fit.'

'What a thing to say! I might change my mind about marrying you.'

Charlie grinned. 'Nah, you love my cakes too much. Plus I'm friends with one of the best chocolate makers in the country. No contest.'

'Do you really think I'm that easy?' Fran plopped her hands on her hips and struggled to glare at him while trying to suppress a bubble of laughter.

'No way.' He held up his hands. 'It's more than my life's worth.'

'Good. For heaven's sake, open that bottle of champagne and feed me chocolate.'

'Your wish is my command.' Charlie proceeded to work his magic, and Fran took a glass from his outstretched hand. The bubbles tickled her nose as she took a sip, and then reached for the nearest chocolate. As the velvety dark chocolate truffle blossomed on her tongue, she met Charlie's megawatt smile. She wished she could stop the world, draw a deep breath, and snapshot this moment. Instead she sent up a silent word of thanks to Agatha Christie.

24

'So you think you're good enough to marry my daughter?'

'Daddy! For goodness sake.' Fran's heated blush drew a smile out of Charlie, but Jack Miller's stern expression didn't soften, so he quickly hid his amusement.

'It's okay. Doesn't offend me.' Charlie linked his hand with hers. 'It's his job to look out for you.'

He'd left Robbie in charge of the shop and met Fran and her father in the Green Man for a late lunch. Even if they hadn't walked in together, their relationship would've been obvious. They shared the same tall lean build, sharp green eyes and sweep of dark hair, although in Jack's case his was heavily streaked with grey and starting to recede.

'I'm probably not good enough, sir,

but I love her with all my heart and will do my absolute best to make her happy.' Charlie's honesty struck home and he received the faintest hint of approval. 'I know Fran's pleased you've accepted the job in Plymouth and will be coming to live nearby.'

'Are you pleased too?' Jack's eyes twinkled.

'Of course.' Charlie decided to risk a joke. 'We'll be fine, as long as you stay on your side of the Tamar River.'

'Maybe you'll do for her after all.' He chuckled and nodded at Fran. 'Your mother would've liked him.' His voice cracked.

'Yes, she would.'

'What was she like? I wish I could've met her.' Charlie's question made them both stare. 'I lost my twin brother a couple of years ago and always hate it when people avoid mentioning Alex for fear of upsetting me.'

'It's much appreciated, Charlie.' Jack grasped his shoulder. 'Pamela was an amazing woman. Good-looking. Smart.

Sharp sense of humour. She'd have roared at your dumb joke.' He shook his head. 'I miss her every day.' For a few seconds he struggled to speak. 'Enough of being sad. We're here to celebrate. Are your family coming to join us?'

'I'm afraid not. My dad's arthritis is playing up today, but maybe you'd like to come to the house tonight? Fran could invite Patrick and Lucy along too. And then there's Robbie. He's — '

'Fran's told me all about the lad, and I'd love to meet everyone. I haven't seen Lucy since she was in pigtails, and I've never met her husband.'

'Great. We'll get it all organised. Is it time to order our lunch?'

'The food's pretty good, Dad, but not quite up to Charlie's standards,' Fran joked.

'It's one of the reasons she's marrying me. I did hear she's not exactly a star in the kitchen.' That earned him a glare from his new fiancée and a broad smile from his future father-in-law

— on balance, not a bad result.

'Her mother hated cooking too, and when I was at sea I'm pretty sure they lived on fish fingers and baked beans. I taught myself to cook so we wouldn't starve.'

'Have you two quite finished denigrating the Miller ladies' culinary skills?'

'I do believe it's time we shut up.' Charlie laughed and passed the menus around.

'Good idea,' Jack agreed. 'I'm guessing we'll be talking wedding plans tonight?'

Fran noticed his panicked glance. 'I hate to tell you this, Charlie, but that's what happens next. I'm guessing you hadn't thought past the proposal?'

'Don't worry,' Jack said. 'Leave it to her and agree with everything she dreams up. Simplest way.'

'Good idea. I'd love to have the ceremony at Truro Cathedral. Of course it'll be top hat and tails for the men, and I think about ten bridesmaids should be perfect,' Fran mused.

Charlie's blood turned to ice before he suddenly registered her satisfied smile, verging on a smirk. She'd got her revenge for his kitchen gibe. 'Very funny, I'm sure.'

'I thought so too.' Fran laughed and turned to include her father. 'Yes, we'll make plans tonight, but I think we'd both prefer something quiet and simple.' She focused back on Charlie. 'Right?'

Somehow he managed to nod and received a kiss for his wise response.

'You're learning. Now let's eat.'

★ ★ ★

'Where've Charlie and my dad disappeared to?' Fran asked. 'Car-ogling, I suppose?'

Lucy rolled her eyes. 'That's a stupid question. Patrick and Robbie tagged along too, and George somehow dragged himself out of the chair because he didn't want to be left out.'

'A cool 1964 Triumph TR4 tops boring wedding plans any day.'

'Or baby talk.' She lowered herself into the nearest chair with a sigh. 'Oh, I'm sorry.' Lucy put her hand to her mouth, 'I didn't mean to — '

'It's all right. Charlie's mum knows.'

'But I . . . I've been selfish, droning on nonstop about the baby — '

'Quite right too,' Fran said firmly. 'I'd hate you to be awkward around me. I'm genuinely thrilled for you and Patrick. Does it hurt sometimes? Of course it does. But Charlie's helped me see it's not the end of the world. He loves me as I am, and we've got definite plans to have a family together — just in a different way than yours.' Fran reached for Helen's hand. 'He's a truly wonderful man, and that's all down to you.'

'Alex and Charlie were the two best boys a mother could have.' Helen's quiet sadness broke Fran's heart. 'I'm so grateful to Charlie for moving back and not simply because of the shop. I don't know how I'd have got through . . . ' Fresh tears stained her cheeks, and Fern wrapped her arms around the older woman. Lucy joined in, and the three of them clung together, drawing strength from each other.

'Wow, is that ever a cool . . . ' Jack strode into the room and came to an abrupt stop. 'What's wrong?'

'Oh, you know how we women get about weddings. All the talk of dresses and flowers upsets the hormones.' Lucy smiled and shrugged it off.

Fran avoided looking at her father. Last night he'd asked if Charlie knew about her surgery and been relieved when she answered in the affirmative. For years, her parents had tried to reassure her that to the right man it wouldn't be an obstacle, but deep down she'd never quite believed them. She suspected it was why she'd always kept her relationships casual, never getting serious enough with any boyfriend to get as far as discussing a future together. One evening she'd almost told Randy, but something had held her back; and when he'd let her down, she knew she'd made the right decision. With Charlie it'd quickly become a question of when to tell him, not if.

The rest of the men piled back into the room, and Charlie instantly sought her out. 'Got everything planned yet?'

'Almost. I've booked the cathedral for next Saturday — will that work?' she teased.

'Perfect. Tell me the time and I'll be there.' He winked at Robbie. 'Ever worn a top hat and tails?'

The boy reddened before catching sight of his mentor's wicked grin. 'You're a nutter.' He shook his head at Fran. 'You must need your head tested, marrying him.'

She wound her arms around Charlie's neck. 'Yep, you're probably right. Don't worry, Robbie, one day some girl will twist you up in knots as well.'

'No way,' he protested.

Charlie's raspy laugh filled the room.

'I used to say the same thing.'

'Tell him you're glad you broke your own rule,' Fran prompted.

'Oh, yeah, right. Whatever she said.' His swift agreement made everyone laugh.

Her eyes stung with fresh tears, despite the fact she'd sworn to get through the rest of the day with her emotions intact. From fleeing a book that refused to be written, she'd ended up writing the next chapter of her mythical autobiography. Fran couldn't wait to see what came next in the story.

25

The next summer on a hot Italian beach

'Are you ever afraid we're too lucky?' Fran mused, fiddling with her shiny new wedding ring.

'Nope.' Charlie propped up on his elbows and slipped off his sunglasses to squint at her. 'We've had our troubles before now, and I'm sure there'll be more down the road, but that's how life goes. It's the old swings and round-abouts, isn't it?'

'You're right.'

'Hey, be careful, sweetheart. I thought those were words no wife ever uttered.'

She playfully smacked his arm and he made a grab for her, yanking her down to him.

'Behave yourself, Mrs. Boscawen.'

Mrs. Boscawen. Fran had kept her

'quiet and simple' promise. Three days ago, they had stood in front of an intimate group of their family and friends at the tiny village church in Tresidder and pledged their love for each other. No top hat and tails. No bridesmaids. And only Alexandre as the world's most adorable pageboy. After the brief ceremony, they'd walked hand in hand through the street while their guests and locals and visitors alike cheered them on, all the way to Anna's chocolate shop.

'Are you dreaming about that chocolate fountain again?' Charlie teased. He toyed with the ends of her hair, now returned to its regular glossy brunette shade, and brushing her bare shoulders.

'What else would I be dreaming about? It was out of this world.'

'Um, maybe the man who baked the lemon and lavender wedding cake of your dreams? Your handsome, charming, talented husband.'

'Oh, that one!' Gazing into his sparkling eyes, the vivid blue of the

Mediterranean sky above their heads, she couldn't resist kissing him. The taste of pistachio gelato lingered on his warm lips and she licked it off.

'You always know how to get around me, don't you?' Charlie's husky voice betrayed his emotions.

'Of course.' Fran sat back up and gazed out over the sea. 'If you keep staring at me, you'll miss the sunset.' He shifted and wrapped her around with his arms and legs, his breath warm on her neck.

'I'd miss this more.'

A delicious tremble ran through her as Charlie's fingers brushed aside her hair to nuzzle her sun-kissed skin. 'Me too.'

'By the way, I checked my phone while I was getting our ice creams.'

'But we agreed we weren't — '

Charlie eased her around to face him and gently covered her mouth with his own, kissing her into silence. 'I know we did, but I'm pretty sure you've been wondering about a certain thing ever since we left Heathrow.' A slow satisfied smile crept over his face. 'You were at number two when we took off, but I'm very pleased to inform you that the new Mrs. Charles Boscawen, aka F. E. Miller, is now a number-one bestseller for the very first time. She totally hit the jackpot all around this week.'

'Oh my God, you're kidding!'

'I wouldn't dare.' He grinned. 'You might sneak me into *Death in December* as a rotting corpse if I don't behave myself.'

'You're a star.' Fran flung her arms around him. 'Thank you so much for checking.' She sat back and studied him carefully. 'What else is going on? There's something you're not telling me.'

'You want more good news? Greedy lady.'

'Charles Michael Boscawen, spill the beans before you get in real trouble.'

'Ooh, I'm scared,' he chuckled. 'All right. Calm down. Don't get mad. There was a message from the adoption agency to say they've set up an appointment with us after we get back.'

'Seriously?'

'Now I definitely wouldn't joke about that, would I?'

It meant too much to them both. Despite Fran's determination to stay upbeat, it'd still been a challenge when little Ewan was born. She'd shared Lucy and Patrick's joy and happily become Ewan's doting godmother, but the tinge of sadness never quite left her alone. 'You know I adore Alexandre and Ewan — '

'Not quite the same though, is it?' Charlie cradled her face with his large hands. 'I promised we'd make our own family, and we are. But we've got to be patient. They said it'll take a while.'

'I know.' She rested against him and drew strength from his certainty. 'Was there anything from Robbie?'

'Yes; he said everything's fine. Chantelle's a big hit, apparently.'

They'd had the brilliant idea of asking Alex's widow to help Robbie take care of the shop while they were away, and it'd given Charlie's parents the priceless gift of time with their adored grandson as a bonus.

'I wish Robbie's family were more . . . supportive.' The teenager had taken it hard when his mother had married Brian Dalby. 'How do you think he'll get on back at school in September?'

'I think he'll be fine with us backing him up. It'll be a different kind of tough after working, but no reputable culinary school will accept him if he doesn't stick it out and get at least a few qualifications under his belt.'

'You'll miss him.'

'I certainly will. He'll still work on weekends and school holidays for a while, and I told him there'll always be a job for him at Boscawen's Bites.'

'You wouldn't want to go back to owning a proper restaurant?'

'No way.' He stroked his hand down to cup her chin. 'I've found out what's really important now, and a Michelin star doesn't make the cut. It's spending time with the people I love, making a difference in the community and having a settled home.' He brushed her lips with a soft kiss. 'And top of the list is doing it all with you.'

'You're top of my list too. I don't need any bestsellers with you in my life.'

'Nice though, isn't it?'

'Of course,' Fran admitted with a broad smile.

She settled back into his arms, and together they watched another glorious sunset, determined to make the most of every single one they were fortunate enough to share.

We do hope that you have enjoyed reading this large print book.

Did you know that all of our titles are available for purchase?

We publish a wide range of high quality large print books including:
Romances, Mysteries, Classics
General Fiction
Non Fiction and Westerns

Special interest titles available in large print are:
The Little Oxford Dictionary
Music Book, Song Book
Hymn Book, Service Book

Also available from us courtesy of Oxford University Press:
Young Readers' Dictionary
(large print edition)
Young Readers' Thesaurus
(large print edition)

For further information or a free brochure, please contact us at:
Ulverscroft Large Print Books Ltd.,
The Green, Bradgate Road, Anstey,
Leicester, LE7 7FU, England.
Tel: (00 44) 0116 236 4325
Fax: (00 44) 0116 234 0205

Other titles in the
Linford Romance Library:

LOVE WILL FIND A WAY

Miranda Barnes

Convalescing after a car accident, Gwen Yorke leases a remote cottage on the beautiful Isle of Skye. She hopes to find inspiration there for her career as a rug designer, and wants to decide if she and her boyfriend have a future together. In Glenbrittle, she finds herself drawn to the enigmatic, moody Andrew McIver, and his young daughter Fiona. To Gwen's delight, she and Fiona become close, frequently sketching together. But why is Andrew so unhappy about their friendship?

THE PRINCE'S BRIDE

Sophie Weston

One of three royal brothers in the Adriatic principality of San Michele, Prince Jonas works hard. But after a protocol-ridden evening, he's due some downtime in his beloved forest. Hope Kennard was the daughter of the manor back in England. But she has guarded her heart since her childhood ended in financial scandal. She's just passing through San Michele, before moving on to another country, another job. But then a charming forest ranger appears. And this time, her instincts don't help . . .

THE UNEXPECTED GIFT

Sarah Purdue

When London nurse Megan Falstaff is informed she's received an inheritance from her beloved godmother Cathleen, she's expecting a couple of cat figurines. What she actually inherits is a boarding cattery in the village of Little River — with the stipulation that she must run it for at least a year. Getting to grips with the eccentricities of felines and village folk alike is challenging for Megan — and matters aren't helped by the disdain of the haughty vet Doctor William Wakefield . . .

ONLY TRUE IN FAIRY TALES

Christine Stovell

Eloise Blake has been fascinated by Prospect House, the shadowy romantic Gothic edifice opposite hers, ever since she moved to the village of Hookfield. When its new owner turns out to be bestselling crime author Ross Farrell, whose work is grounded in gritty reality rather than happy endings, she is determined to concentrate on her tapestry design business and her rescue dog Gracie. Love, she thinks, is only true in fairy tales. But is Ross the Prince Charming she thought didn't exist — or is he a beast in disguise?

THE MAGIC CHARM

Christina Green

When Goldie Smith spies the portrait of the three Crosby girls for the first time, belonging to her dear Great-aunt Mary and painted long ago by an enigmatic local artist, she can't help but wonder at the history behind it. She also takes an instant shine to Rob Tyson, the handsome man who comes to photograph the painting. But his first love seems to be the rare birds he makes extensive trips to record with his camera. Is there room for Goldie in his life as well?